THE
JOURNALS OF
BETH JORDACHE

THE
JOURNALS OF
BETH JORDACHE

Adapted from
Phil Redmond's Brookside
by
Rachel Braverman

B⊞XTREE

The publishers would like to thank the following
for their help and advice in producing this book:

Phil Redmond
Philip Reevell
Brookside Producer Mal Young
Brookside Script Editor Gareth Brookes

First published in Great Britain in 1994 by
Boxtree Limited
Broadwall House, 21 Broadwall, London SE1 9PL

ISBN 0 7522 0972 8

10 9 8 7 6 5 4 3 2

A CIP catalogue entry for this book is available
from the British Library

Typeset by SX Composing Ltd, Rayleigh, Essex
Printed in Great Britain by
Cox & Wyman Ltd, Reading, Berks

A MERSEY TELEVISION COMPANY

Brookside

12th February 1993

'Daddy's little girl.'

My eyes sprang open. I woke up sweating, screaming. In my nightmares, I can't outrun him.

It's always him I dream about. I hate that! During the day, it's alright, I can cope. But at night *he* takes over.

And all I can do is scream . . . and scream . . . and scream . . .

Go away. Get away from us. Leave us alone. Haven't you caused enough damage?

Mum was there before I'd even opened my eyes, hugging me tight, she keeps telling me –

We're safe here.
We're safe here.
We're safe here.

Over and over again she said It. I just hope she's right. But I still don't believe it.

He's in prison and this is a safe house. A *safe* house. No-one in Brookside Close knows who we are.

Morning

One of the neighbours called round about the noise. If only I could sleep properly. I didn't want Mum to open the door, but she said they'd be even more nosy if they thought there was some big mystery about us.

She only went and told them our name! Apparently everyone thinks the house has been bought by a Mrs. Shackleton, but they'd never seen her, so we could have become the Shackletons. Simple. Trust Mum to miss the obvious solution. Mandy Shackleton and her daughters, Beth and Rachel. It's not bad. Better than Jordache.

His name. Without it, we could be free of him. Well, freer. It would make it harder for him to find us, at least.

You'd have thought it would be easy to be anonymous in a city, but not in Brookside Close. Every time we collect the milk off the doorstep, the net curtains are twitching. Why won't they leave us alone? Mum says they're just being friendly.

She said we should be glad people around here are so concerned. Who's she trying to kid? I know she's worried, but as usual, she pretends everything's going to work out.

We're fine on our own. We don't need anyone else. Better off without them.

Rachel thinks I'm overreacting. She doesn't know the half of it – I hope she never does. Sometimes I wish I was thirteen again, like her. All innocence and trusting.

She'll learn.

Oh God, please don't let her find out the hard way. Like I did.

There's so much I can never tell anyone. I can't have a normal life with ordinary friends, because of him.

Mum's been going on at me again about wearing black all the time, saying I should brighten myself up. I'm happy wearing black. It keeps people out. No-one can tell anything about me.

22nd February 1993

Mum's had an accident, scalded her leg. We were only trying to cheer her up – breakfast in bed. Things were going so well, too. It's hard to believe we've only been here a couple of weeks. Mum's made it look like a proper home, all these pieces of china and stuff. Some of them are a bit naff, but she's trying.

My room's great and Rachel's never out of hers! I've started at college. Rachel's at the local school and Mum's got friendly with the neighbours – Jean Crosbie and Patricia Farnham. Mum likes them. They're alright, I suppose . . .

I was actually beginning to think we could be a normal family. There's loads round here that are one parent. We'd blend in OK. We've even got to know the window cleaner. Cosy, or what! His name's Sinbad. No second name. He's a bit of a gossip. I'm sure he only climbs his ladder to look in people's windows.

A couple of times, he's come round and offered to help out if we need anything. He's a laugh. Got a mad sense of humour, does all these impressions. I like him.

Last night, I actually slept right through. So did Mum. She was still snoring away when I got up, so I decided to get her breakfast in bed with proper coffee. The tray looked brilliant with a flower and everything. I couldn't believe how fast asleep she was. She was dead chuffed when I woke her up. It's great when she smiles like that.

Then, I don't know how, the coffee went flying, all over Mum's legs. They went bright red. It looked horrible, especially with the marks He'd left.

She didn't yell or anything. The pain was probably nothing to what He did to her. Rachel had left for school, so I knocked on the window to get her to come back and give me a hand. Jean Crosbie came with her. She said she used to be a nurse, so at least Mum got proper treatment.

I tried to stop her from seeing Mum's legs. I promised I'd

call a doctor. I was so scared and ashamed when she lifted Mum's skirt and saw the other scars. Poor Mum! She looked like death.

God knows what Jean Crosbie thought. Mum made something up about another accident. No way Jean believed her. There she was, being so nice about it, and all I wanted was for her to go. As soon as she left, I put the chain on the door.

I'm being stupid. I know that really. He has no power over me now. He can't touch any of us from where he is. Perhaps if I keep writing it and saying it and thinking it, I'll actually start to believe it.

Mum told Jean he was dead. Another lie. We don't even tell the truth to each other.

26th February 1993

They've actually let him go! He's out on parole. How could they? After all he's done, he's only been there for two pathetic years. After all the misery and harm and damage he's done.

I bet he charmed the parole board into releasing him. That smile. People always think he's so wonderful, until they find out the truth. Most of them never do. They'll think Mum made it all up or exaggerated. Bet she was asking for it . . .

Mrs. Shackleton came round to tell us. I don't know whether I'm glad or sorry that she did. But there's no way he'd fool her. She understands what Mum's been through.

But she doesn't know about me. I wish I could tell her, but Mum would hate it if I did. So would I.

It's like this big unspoken thing between us. Me and Mum

talk about everything else, except that, the most important thing in my life. Sometimes I want to shake her until she admits what really went on.

I can't though. She's been hurt too much already, I mustn't make it worse. There's no-one else to look after her.

I can feel panic burning in my stomach. Then I get angry . . . really angry. It's good when that happens. As long as I stay angry, I'm okay. But now he's on the loose, the fear's coming back.

I'm glad we found out from Mrs. Shackleton. What if he'd just turned up on the doorstep? Hello, darling, I'm home. What about a kiss for your old Dad? Daddy's little girl.

15th March 1993

Mum's really been on edge lately. I thought it was her nerves, but it was him. Somehow he got hold of our address. He came to find us. I always knew he would. Mum saw him. He sent her flowers. Said he'd keep coming back.

Then he was waiting for me at college this afternoon. It was a nightmare. I couldn't believe he was actually standing there.

I ran back into college, but he ran after me, chased me down the corridor. He said he only wanted to talk. I told him to get lost. He started to go, then turned round with that awful sincere look on his face. That smile . . . those eyes . . . Five minutes, Beth, he said. It's his favourite trick! Why do I fall for it?

Every time.

Every time.

I should have kept my mouth shut until he'd gone. But

there was this stupid hope inside me that maybe he might have changed. Changed! Him!? What was I thinking?!

It was so normal. Pretending he was really concerned about me. Like I was some sulky teenager, worried about homework or spots or something. He was so sweet and understanding and nice. He makes me sick.

But I decided I wasn't going to let him get to me. I won't let him near me, physically *or* mentally.

He said he was sorrier than I could imagine. Dead right. I can't imagine him being sorry at all. Everything he says has a double meaning. On the surface, it seems so honest. Underneath there's a twist. I told him he didn't know me any more. "I do", he said and I felt his eyes could look right inside me. Remember the anger. Keep him out. Remember the anger.

Then he told me he'd seen Mum. He went on about asking for forgiveness, and how he'd changed.

"I believe there's real hope," he said in that awful soft voice.

I told him no chance, to go to hell and leave us alone. But Mum's so weak with him. She'll fall for the same old lines . . . that smile.

REMEMBER!!!
Remember what he did and hate him.
REMEMBER THE ANGER

It's the only way out. If only he'd go and never come back, we might stand a chance at leading some kind of a life.

I couldn't stop crying and shaking when I got home. All I could think was that we had to get away. Right away from him.

I started throwing my stuff in a bag. Jeans. Dresses. Socks. Everything.

But Mum stopped me, putting her arms round me and holding me tight. She said we'd be OK, we could stick it out. I want to believe her so much. After a while, I calmed down. We're in this together, Mum and me. We've got this far. We can keep going. Mum helped me to unpack. My drawers are dead tidy now!

17th March 1993

3 AM

My nightmare woke me up again. It's really dark outside. At least I didn't scream the place down. I've said the words, actually said them out loud to Mum. She didn't want to hear. I could see my words hurting her. I didn't care. I was furious. Every time I try to do something a bit ordinary, it's there to slap me down.

Mike Dixon from next door invited me to go out with him and his mates. Four of us. Keith, his flatmate, and Margaret who lives at the Farnhams.

Mike's really nice, not bad looking and fun. Margaret's great. She's from Manchester too, so we've got that in common for a start. She's got great hair, masses of it, red gold and curly. The complete opposite of me.

I didn't want to go at first, because Mum would have to be on her own. She said she'd be fine and virtually pushed me out of the door, although I could see she was worried he might come. There's a look that comes over her face. A smile so fixed you think it's going to shatter. I can always tell. I went anyway. Like Mum said, we can't hide forever.

It was a real laugh. We went bowling and Mike was *definitely* chatting me up. He's so obvious. I told him I wanted to be a paediatrician. He was dead impressed – when he knew what a pædiatrician is.

Mum asked if I was going to go out with him again. As if I could with all the other things on my mind. She made out it was because I was worried about revision.

Revision!!!

I've told Rachel that he's out of prison. She was dead upset – she misses him a lot. Mum said it was the idea of having a Dad. I'm not so sure. Rachel still thinks he's wonderful. Is it better for her to stay in the dark and carry on loving him? Or should I tell her the truth?

Sometimes I want her to know every last detail, why I hate him so much. But she's the only one in this family he hasn't ruined.

Mum was furious with me at first. Later on, she apologised. I'm so sick of the endless secrets. Then Mum made me really mad. She said that she missed him too. Missed having a man around. Man? He's no man! He's an animal.

If I write the dream down, maybe it'll go away.

I'm lying asleep in my old bed in my old room. I'm having a nightmare within the nightmare.

A voice calls me.

"Beth."
"Wake up."
"You're dreaming."

I open my eyes, glad it's over. He's standing over me. With

that smile on his face. That smile. The voice doesn't sound as if it comes from him. It's still so gentle and soft.

"Beth."
"Let me in."
"Daddy wants to come in."

I don't want to, but I have no choice. My hands pull back the covers. I can't stop them. He's in control. In control of my body. I'm just his puppet.

"Beth."
"I'm cold."
"Make Daddy warm."

His hands are on my arms, pinning me down. They're so hot they burn. I can feel my skin blistering under his palms. He trembles like a dog.

I try to scream, but he's got my voice as well. He bears down on me, crushing me. To death. The weight's too much. I'm choking silently and I can't breathe.

All the time the voice goes on and on.

"Don't worry."
"I'm cold."
"It won't hurt."
"I love you."

He's pressing down, heavier and heavier. It's my last chance to save myself. I open my mouth and scream and scream. At last, I manage to wake myself up.

But what if I don't?

What if one night, I can't wake up in time?

11th March 1993

There was a single red rose in the sink when I came home today. I knew right away who it was from.

Typical! He thinks he can get what he wants with a few hearts and flowers. The trouble is, he could be right. Mum said a big bunch came a week ago. She ripped it to shreds and put it in the bin before I could see it. Now this disgusting rose appears.

She let it sit there. In our sink. Drinking our water.

I blew my top. Tore it apart. Ripped it into tiny pieces. How could she have it in the house? Contaminating us with his evil.

She refuses to see what's happening. Just one flower, she said. It's far more than that. She's letting him back in, bit by bit. Flower by flower.

I've seen it all before. Why can't Mum? It's just like the bad old days. Now, he's turned on the charm, so sweet and kind, such a loving husband – until he's sure he's got us all hooked again. Then it'll be the same as before. Bruises in the morning, screaming at night and never, ever letting the neighbours hear.

And it's working! She brought out a letter from him. The post mark was Liverpool. He's living here in some kind of hostel. He'll never leave us alone now that he's practically on the doorstep.

The letter was *good*. I'll give him that. A masterpiece of sweet talk. He said how much he was missing us and how he loved us.

Love. Love. Love.

He's so generous with that word. Six times on one page!

But it's another of his double meanings. "I love you, Beth, so I'm going to have you."

Mum came out with the usual – "This time it'll be different. This time he's changed. This time he means it." Yeah – like he did all the other times!

I had to do something to stop him, so I said I'd leave if he set foot in this house. Our so-called 'safe' house. Then the truth came out.

"If we fight him too hard, he could do anything," she said. And she meant it. He might snatch Rachel from school. Corrupt her too. She's got that right, at least. He seems so straight, but he's so devious. He only went to prison before because even he can't disguise broken ribs and a ruptured spleen.

I can hardly remember those two days while Mum was unconscious. I think I spent the whole time cuddling Rachel and trying not to cry. I can't picture the faces of the social workers at the home, there's nothing there. Just a blur. It's only his face I see. Sharp in my dreams. Two years haven't changed him. Nothing can.

I don't know what to do. I can't really go. It would mean leaving Mum and Rachel in his clutches. Perhaps I should tell Mrs. Shackleton, but then we'd be chucked out of the house. Mum would never forgive me.

Besides, if he can find us here, he can find us anywhere. There's the police, but what can they do? Take him away? He'd only come back.

I hate myself when I get like this. As bad as Mum – giving up. All I can do is give her the choice – him or me. I just hope she loves me enough to *Keep Him Out!*

22nd March 1993

Saw a film with Mike tonight. We had a really good laugh. Except he went on about how romantic my Dad is, sending Mum flowers – if he only knew.

His Mum runs the flower shop. *She's* really fallen for him. That smile Apparently he told her about the drink, how he'd been to Alcoholics Anonymous and they cured him. Then he had the nerve to say he'd rediscovered his faith. Faith! It's news to me!

He's such a con artist. He really must have turned on the charm.

He blames it all on demon drink or on someone winding him up. Anything, except himself. Am I the only person who can see through him? Behind that smile.

I don't know how anyone can believe in God. If He existed, Dad'd be in hell. Not charming the neighbours and making our lives a misery. I notice he didn't admit to Mrs. Dixon that he'd raped his own daughter. Or that he beat Mum so badly she was in hospital for weeks. He always knows just how far to go.

Mike Dixon's alright. He seems really nice, so I took a big chance and told him the truth. Not the whole truth – a bit of it. I said Dad had got two years for beating up Mum. He was shocked, but he didn't run off. I'm glad I did tell him. I'm going to need a friend. I made him promise not to tell anyone.

Sometimes, I want to shout it from the rooftops, so he can't fool anyone ever again. But then, everyone would know. Wherever I went, people would point. The girl who went to bed with her father. Her father, the one who went to prison for assaulting her mother.

I want people to know who I am, but if they knew about my past, that's all I'd be to them. A victim, an abused body, not a real person.

Then there's the others.

"She was asking for it."

"Jail bait."

"She knew what she was doing."

"She led him on."

"It was her own fault."

You see it on the telly when they report how judges let rapists off. It would be different if I'd been a little kid, but I was fourteen. Old enough to know better. Only I didn't. I believed him, like everyone else.

29th March 1993

He's actually been inside this house!

I knew this would happen! I knew it! It's all Mum's fault, said she had to talk to him in person. If she's to stop running away from him, she has to face up to the past. She actually wanted to find out how much of it was her fault. As if any of it could be! He's got her right where he wants her. Hooked and terrified! Ready for him to reel her in, so he can start beating her head in again.

He promised to keep away. I knew that wouldn't last two minutes. She always lets him back. As usual, she swore it would be different this time. The worst thing is, she means it every time. She's not like him, lying for the sake of it, but she gives in. In her own mind, she's convinced he's changed. How can she be so blind?

Rachel was fourteen today. Mum made her a special tea. Then he came with a present. When I got back from college he was standing in the lounge. Polluting the atmosphere.

Rachel was thrilled, of course. Her Dad. He bought her this poxy T-shirt. Mum got chocolates. She wouldn't take the box, so Rachel had them as well. It'll serve her right if she ends up weighing 20 stone!

I wouldn't speak to him. I wouldn't even look at him. He tried to make it seem so ordinary. So nice. A big family gathering. How touching!

"Here's my big daughter," he said.

I'm not his *anything* any more. Rachel is, though. She was so pleased to see him. Loved the present. It didn't matter to her what it was – it was from her Dad.

I made Mum tell him to leave. Rachel was crying and carrying on. She thinks I'm just being heartless. How can I explain? Better she hates me than that she finds out the truth.

She hasn't taken the T-shirt off, even for bed.

Still, he went without a fuss after I said I'd go to the police if he ever came near us again. I mean it. This time, I *really* mean it. I don't care if we do have to move again.

The battle's between him and me now. It would be so easy to give in. He'd come back. For a few days everything would be fine. Rachel would be pleased, Mum would go on about how wonderful the change in him is.

Then something will happen – or nothing. He'll lose his temper and it'll all start up again. There's no way I'm going to let history repeat itself.

Mum knew I meant it too. I've lost count of the number of times she's promised me he'd never come anywhere near us. But he was in the house today.

He disappeared round the corner. Mum slipped out of the front door after him. I listened from the door. If she'd invited him back, I'd have gone. I know I would. She knows I would.

I think I might finally have got through to her. She told him she wanted a divorce. Good! Right there on the step. So he went through the whole bit again. How he loved her. How he'd changed. How deep down she loved him too. That smile.

Mum stood her ground. I was really proud of her. Her voice was quiet, like it always is, but there was no mistaking her meaning.

"It's best for all our sakes," she said.

If there is a god up there,
    please
        please
            make her go through with it this time.

5th April 1993

Once he got out, it was inevitable. First the big bunch of flowers, then the romantic single rose, then Rachel's awful birthday tea. He's made a plan and there's nothing I can do to stop him carrying it out.

I've done what I could. I didn't let him get round me that time he turned up at college. He can't get round me, but he's coming to stay.

He's told Mum some pathetic sob story of how someone broke into his bedsit at the hostel. Stole the one possession he had. It was a watch Mum gave him once. I remember it. She'd had it engraved – 'Tick tock, Trev's clock'.

She went on about how awful his room was and what a state he was in. Poor, poor Dad. My heart bleeds for him!

I really lost my rag. I told her how stupid she was being. She promised faithfully she'd never have him back.

"It's only for two days."

Two days! Who does she think she's kidding!!

Am I the only person in the world who can see what's going on? Sometimes I feel like I'm living at right angles to the rest of the human race. No-one else looks at things from where I'm standing.

Mum keeps changing her promises. She'll never admit that she's broken them. She must realise, deep down, that she knows he's not going to change. That she's making promises she won't keep.

I was all set to phone the Shackletons. My hand was on the dial. They'd have been able to talk some sense into her. Mum stopped me. That look on her face always gets to me – defeated and scared. She begged me not to phone. They'd throw us out and then what would we do.

One more chance. One final promise, and he'll be out of our lives forever. For her sake, I put the phone down again. The worst thing is that he's right. In her heart of hearts, she *does* want him back. She wants him back more than she wants me to be safe. Perhaps the years of me looking after her have made her forget I need looking after too sometimes.

I'm as bad as Mum in a way. How many times have I said "I mean it"? Hundreds. Thousands. Millions, even. I could have called the Shackletons. I could have called the police. But I didn't. Does that mean I'm weak like Mum or calculating like Dad?

Mum says Dad's the weak one. He's OK until something winds him up. It doesn't take much to do that. He'll never change, whether he wants to or not.

I should have phoned. I could phone now. I could go down the stairs and pick up the receiver and dial. I could stop him coming. Just a couple of days, she said. Till he sorts himself out. Give him one more chance. She'll never forgive me if I don't.

Mike Dixon's asked me to the cinema again tonight. He's picking me up in an hour. I'm not going to hang around, playing happy families.

That was the doorbell!

Dad's here.

7th April 1993

4 AM (Mike Dixon's house)

I'm lying on a couch in the living room of a strange house. My teeth won't stop chattering, I'm so cold.

He's on the other side of the wall, sleeping on the sofa, breathing our air. How am I supposed to sleep when he's so close? This is the second night I've been next door. I can't go back.

It was alright staying last night. I couldn't face going home after the film. Mike said I could stay at his place, if the landlord agreed. What a surprise that was! I was imagining some old bloke in a cardigan. Peter Harrison's nothing like that.

He's dead good looking, a couple of years older than Mike but tall, dark and handsome, with eyes to die for. . . . Writing about him makes me feel better. Mike's nothing by comparison. He's dead relaxed. You can trust Peter just by looking at him. (I know that's rubbish really – people trust Dad all the time. Peter's different.)

I'm not the only one who thinks he's alright. There's a girl sharing the house as well, Anna. I think she's Polish or something. She kept making excuses to be with Peter. I don't think he's all that struck on her though.

How long has it been since I thought about anything as ordinary as who fancies who? What is Dad doing to me? What's he doing to Mum and Rachel while I'm not there?

I went back this morning. I thought he'd have had the decency to keep out during the day. No matter how low my expectations of him are, he goes lower. Not only was he there, but Mum had gone out.

It was exactly what I'd been dreading. Him and me, eyeball to eyeball. My first instinct was to run, then I thought no. No!

Maybe Mum's right and the way to get rid of him is to face him. Head on.

He is so predictable! I was armed against the I-want-us-to-be-a-family bit. It won't wash with me. He said how concerned he was. How he cared because he's my father.

Then he came out with "deep down you want me back". I've heard those words so often, they don't mean a thing any more. I know what I feel inside. Remember the anger. There's a solid core of hate and disgust. I used to turn it against myself, but now it's all there to use against him.

"You raped me."

He denied it. What else was it? Incest? Fooling around? Interfering with me?

"One weak moment". That's what he called it. As if all the pain and guilt and fear were nothing.

He ruined my life and then says it was just one weak moment. All the nights I lay awake terrified in case he came back. What about the nightmares? He goes on and on about prison, but what about *my* prison? I'm stuck inside my body, stuck with the knowledge of what he's done and nobody can give me parole.

He tried to tell me he'd had treatment in prison. Does he really think I'm so stupid? How could he have treatment for something nobody knows about. He went to prison for beating up his wife, not for raping his daughter.

I had to get away from him. I ran next door. It was as if they were expecting me. The walls are so thin, they could probably hear us shouting. Of course, he came after me and started hammering on the door. Mike, Peter and Anna were brilliant. Especially Peter!

They didn't ask any questions. Anna took me into the back and Mike answered the door. For a minute, I was frightened that Dad would get past him, he's terrifying when he wants to be. Then Peter spoke to him. He said he'd call the police if Dad didn't go.

But then – once again – that smile, the charm. "No harm done – sorry to bother you." When he was gone Peter said I was welcome to the couch – my own safe house.

Now, I don't know what to do. While he was in prison, I'd started to forget what the real horror was. Worse than the actual rape in a way. It was the quiet moments, like when he kissed me and it wasn't what a father's supposed to do or a big smacker for a birthday. Almost on the lips. He was always touching me – putting his arm round me and squeezing just a bit too tight.

I hated that because it felt alright, but *not* alright. He made me feel wanted, like I was the favourite. It wasn't wrong, exactly. But it wasn't right either. When he finally did it, I knew all the rest was bad too. Where should I have drawn the line? Fathers kiss their daughters all the time. They don't all sleep with them.

13th April 1993

How long can this carry on? There's nothing in my life but Him. Every thought, every action revolves around him.

Will he be there when I get back?

Will he be in a good mood?

Who will he hit?

He's got us right where he wants us. I didn't think it was possible to hate so much.

I've been half living at home, half living next door. It's mad! No kind of life at all. Part of me wants to walk away, forget A levels, forget university, just escape. But I can't let Mum down, she's more trapped than I am. And what about Rachel, who's going to protect her if I'm not there?

I feel watched – threatened. Every minute I'm in here. Our so-called safe house! I've got to stay, though. It's not fair on Mum and Rachel to keep away any longer.

I told him to go. To get out of our lives and stay out! I was so angry.

I pushed him out of the back door, into the rain. Rachel started carrying on, of course. He made himself look so pathetic, letting the drops trickle down his face really laying it on thick.

I know what it's like to trust him. But not now. Why does Mum go on making the same mistake over and over again? Perhaps he's hurt her so much, she can't think straight. I remember when he hit her sometimes. She'd put her hands up, but without really doing anything to lessen the pain. That look. I couldn't stand it. It said, go on. Get it over with. I'm prepared to take my punishment.

I asked for it.

Any minute now it's going to start again. Mum let him back in again. Just for a while etc. etc. He smiled at me. A triumphant, smarmy, "I've won" smile. So I went next door. I couldn't stand being in the house with him another second.

I wouldn't be here now, only Peter persuaded me to come back. It's funny. Although Peter and Mike and Anna know perfectly well what's going on, it's hard to talk about it. There's nothing for me to be ashamed of, but I *am* ashamed. Embarrassed to be such a victim. I want to take control of my own life.

If he found this book, he'd kill me. How many teenagers say that about their parents? But I mean it literally. If he saw how many secrets I've let out in these pages, he'd hit me and hit me until I was dead.

I can't stay here – I'm too scared, but I can't leave either.

20th April 1993

He's back in. Not just in the house. In her bed, too. I brought her a cup of tea and he came out of her room, pretending to be normal. Calling me a good girl. Aren't we the happy family? Just like before.

Did they have sex? Did she enjoy it? Is that what keeps her with him? More likely, he threatened her! I remember listening to someone on the telly once, going on about how some women like being hit. How it turns them on. He should have met my Mum. She doesn't like it – she just doesn't know how to stop it.

Neither do I.

What I hate most about him is his quietness. Even when he's at his most violent, there's hardly a sound. He knows how to hit so his victim groans. Don't scream! Never scream, or the neighbours will hear. His voice is so charming. Every word's a threat.

I don't know what to do. We're all trapped. I ought to phone someone, tell anybody, do something. Is this the way our lives are going to be? Is this forever? The worst thing is, we escaped once. Had a few months of almost freedom. That route's closed off.

Peter and this book are all I've got. He's sympathetic, but he can't actually do a lot. Except listen. Writing things down stops me from shouting them in the street. I can't even talk to Mum about it. That's the worst. The endless pretence that it isn't happening.

23rd April 1993

In a strange way, I was almost relieved to see the bruises. There's the proof, written in black and blue on Mum's body. I was right all along. It was only a matter of time before he started in on her again.

Mum was sitting on the bed, putting on a jumper. She looked really drained and ill. Her arm went up slowly, through the sleeve, then she winced. Her rheumatism playing up again! That's what Dad used to say. He played the concerned and loving husband, taking care of his poor, sick wife.

Everyone believed him.

I've been fooled too. Until I actually saw the marks with my own eyes, there was an outside chance of a hope that he might have changed. How pathetic! Finding out made me stronger. I thought I already hated him as much as I could. I hate him more now.

I was so angry. I was ready to call the Shackletons, but Mum stopped me again. It wouldn't do any good. Mum let him back in. We'd be chucked out of here and left to his mercy. He's got her right under his thumb.

She told me he threatened her. He crept into her bedroom and into her bed. He said he'd kill her, me and Rachel and himself if she didn't do what he said. What had he got to lose, he's already been in prison. If they put him in prison again, he'll come out. With his charm, he'll be on parole before the judge has finished passing sentence!

It was their wedding anniversary that set it all off. Twenty years he's been bullying her, and *he* wanted to celebrate! He insisted. Mum didn't want to go through with it.

Dad invited everyone. Only the Crosbies from across the Close turned up. No way was I going to be there. They left after one drink. He made it too awkward. One minute laughing and the next laying into Mum. Does he really think people don't notice? Trouble is, half the time, they don't – or they pretend they don't.

He blamed her. She showed him up. Her fault.

How did he get so warped? Does he believe his own lies? Sometimes I think he does. Sometimes I think it's just an excuse. He knows perfectly well what's real, but he'd rather hit Mum than sort himself out.

30th April 1993 (At Peter's)

Mike rescued me. It really was a rescue too. All the time we're fighting our battles in number 10, I forget people can hear. Everyone knows what's going on!

Maybe that's why no-one came to the anniversary party. They didn't want to go through the charade of celebrating something so disgusting. Perhaps people are nicer than I thought. Perhaps they were scared of Dad. Or just uncomfortable. When Dad puts on his we're-such-a-happy-family act, what can other people say?

This afternoon, it got too much for me. I've avoided being alone with him as much as I can. Luckily, college is a good excuse.

I misjudged it today, though. Mum was out and Rachel was at school, so he had the place to himself. I should have left as soon as I realised. But I couldn't resist telling him to go. I'll never say anything else to him.

He's not supposed to be here. He's not supposed to come anywhere near us. There's an injunction keeping him away. But if he wants something, nothing's going to get in his way! The police could arrest him just for being in the house. Being within a hundred yards of Mum. If she'd been there, I probably wouldn't have gone near the phone. She would have been too scared to let me.

I got as far as dialling the first two 9s before he ripped the phone out of the wall. Smashed it to the floor, stamping on it . . . into a thousand pieces. Then he really went for me. Held my head in his hands. I didn't know if he was going to kiss me or break my neck. I heard myself screaming. I couldn't stop – if I did, he'd finally kill me.

Let the neighbours hear! Please God, let the neighbours hear. And they did! Mike rang the doorbell. I thought Dad wouldn't answer it, just get on with killing me. But then he let go – to keep up appearances for the neighbours. That smile.

I never was more glad to see Mike standing there. He handled it really well. He played Dad's game. Pretended he was inviting me out for coffee. Just the lad next door asking a normal girl for a date.

It was like watching a play. I was so stunned I could hardly move. I could hardly speak, my throat was so sore and bruised. Dad said something about me having to do revision. I went towards the open door. I knew he'd never dare to stop me with Mike there. I said my revision was OK and I left. Walked straight out of the door with Mike.

3rd May 1993

Every time I think he's done his worst, he goes one step further.

I was at the college library, trying to study. I should never have left them. Not for a moment. But I thought I'd go mad if I didn't get away for a while.

Mike and Peter heard him attacking Mum through the walls. They knew what was happening by the sound of things smashing. He must have pushed her against the dresser. All the ornaments are broken.

Peter called the police, but she sent them away. She was so scared, she pretended everything was OK. Nothing to worry about. Why didn't they insist? How could they possibly have believed such rubbish? It must have been obvious she was lying and he was waiting for her behind the door. Waiting for her to send the police away so that he could carry on beating her.

I went straight home when Peter told me what had happened. Mum was out cold when I finally plucked up the courage to go back. At first, I wondered why she hadn't escaped. Left with the police. Then I remembered Rachel. Mum used to send us to our rooms so we wouldn't see what he was doing. Didn't stop us hearing it, though.

I rushed upstairs. Rachel's door was closed – not a sound. I crept toward it . . . hoping, but something told me it was too late. I reached out. Pushed the door slowly open. The light from the hall fell on to Rachel's bed. I didn't want to cry, but couldn't help it. They were asleep in my sister's bed. It could have been so innocent. A loving father cuddling a child frightened by a nightmare. Maybe she's still innocent, I thought. I hoped. I cried.

When Rachel came downstairs, she was dead pale and kept saying everything was OK. That's how I knew. She wouldn't admit what he did. Couldn't admit it.

Poor Rachel. What did she ever do to deserve that? What could she possibly have done that was so bad she should have a father like him?

She's just a kid. I wish there was some way I could protect her from all this hurt. Thinking about how she was when she was little, all sweet and clumsy, makes me want to cry. She's the complete opposite to me, outgoing, sporty, friendly. I used to be jealous when I was young, but now I'm just proud of her. We've been really close, all three of us. Even her loving Dad is a good sign really. It shows how affectionate she is. I can't bear the thought of what's been destroyed in her.

Remember the anger. I want her to be angry. It's the only way. When he came downstairs, I took her into the extension, out of his way. She didn't say a word. Just sat on the spare bed and stared at the wall.

We could hear him laying into Mum. Not hitting her this time, but grinding her down with his words. How she was poison. How she's evil. How she turns everyone against him. Mum told me once that if something's repeated often enough, you start to believe it. But I'll never believe him. *Not one word.*

I had to go in there, even though it meant leaving Rachel. He called me "darling"! Said they were talking about how important it is that I pass my exams. Does he really think I don't listen? He wanted money off Mum, she didn't have any, so I gave him a fiver, made him take it. Even said please. Anything to get him to go!

He took himself off to get drunk. Peace at last. How many times did we all breathe sighs of relief as he slammed the door. We knew there'd be hell to pay when he got back, but at least the pain stopped for a bit.

As soon as he'd gone, Rachel reappeared. She said she wanted to get out. *Now.* Mum and I tried to get her to talk about what happened.

First, she denied anything happened, but we could see she was covering up. Mum and I said over and over again that it wasn't her fault. I'll never forget what Rachel said next.

"He's my dad and I love him. I don't want him to go away."

But he's got to go if she's ever going to be safe. The man she loves has nothing to do with our father. It's someone she's made up in her head. What he should be like, because the reality's too awful.

I told her he'd done the same thing to me. She just sat there, as if she hadn't heard, crying her heart out.

5th May 1993

We've decided, Mum and I. He's got to go. He'll never stop. It's up to us. There's no other way. We've no choice left.

It's worse for Mum. I don't think he'll dare to rape me again, but how can we keep Rachel out of his way? She's been staying with some friends for the past couple of nights. What's she told them? Dad wanted to know who these people were. He was probably worried that Rachel might say a word out of place. Despite his bullying!

When he came back this afternoon, it was as though he'd never been in prison. It was exactly the same as before. He told me off for wearing black all the time.

I wear black because my mood is black.

I tried to stand up for Mum, but that just makes him worse. He accuses her of poisoning my mind. It's him. He's the poison.

He'd been drinking. He started crying, getting all paranoid. Everyone's out to get him. Everybody's to blame except himself. Then he went quiet. He said he was going to lie down. Mum was supposed to join him, "to comfort him", but she was terrified to go.

I didn't want to cry, to stoop to his level, but I couldn't help it. Mum was trembling so much she could hardly undo her buttons. It was always the same. She'd try to delay climbing the stairs, hoping he'd fall into a stupor before he noticed she hadn't followed him. We sat there, holding our breath, but he didn't call.

Mum's not to blame for any of this. She said she should never have let him back. It's what I've been saying all along, but I could see the power he has over her. How can she simply throw off twenty years of his evil? What hurts her most is the damage he's doing to me and Rachel. She said she could take the beatings, but not us suffering.

We mustn't accept it. We need to be strong, both of us. For Rachel's sake and for our own, we must make sure he never touches her again. Mum and I have come to a decision – we get rid of him. For good.

It's either him – or us.

7th May 1993

OhmyGodohmyGodohmyGod!

He's dead!

We did it. I never thought it would be this hard. It looks so easy in films. One shot and it's all over. Not him. He fought us to the end.

First we had to keep Rachel out of the way. Mum wanted me to steer clear as well. No chance!

Once we'd decided to do it, my head was clear. Poor Mum could hardly stand the terror, but I felt better than I had since he came out of prison. It's always been up to me to be strong for her. My hate is strong enough for anything.

We had some weed killer. Sinbad brought it round. Another of his good turns! I decided to put it in his whiskey. No chance of him tasting anything odd when he's drunk. I even bought him a bottle – how generous of me! He was always saying what a good daughter I was.

We hadn't a clue how much to use. The container just said poison.

He didn't suspect anything. Why should he? He was sprawled out in front of the telly. We watched him from the kitchen counter, like a slow motion action replay. When the stuff went down his throat, I could feel my heart beating faster and faster. Then he coughed and spluttered, as though he was choking. We were so scared we couldn't talk. Not even to each other.

I thought, "Any moment now, he's going to find the poison and kill us." But he didn't. He rampaged through the house. Mum and I sat as still as we could.

Eventually, he went out. Complaining of a stomach ache, but more interested in the booze. We just sat there.

He was away for hours. There was no way of knowing what he was up to. When it got dark, Mum couldn't stand it any more. She had her coat on and was going out to look for him. God knows where she thought she'd start. What if he'd collapsed in front of a policeman? What if someone had taken him to hospital and they'd diagnosed poison?

Mum's hand was actually on the door knob when he fell inside. He was hot and sweating. We watched him lurch to the kitchen sink and stick his head under the tap. All the time, he was shouting and raving about a burning in his stomach. He was furious. Kept shouting for drinks and God knows what. We couldn't move.

Then he disappeared into the extension and the house was silent again. We didn't dare go in. All night long we waited to see if he'd come out. We went through it again and again. He would have killed us in the end. We had to do it – him or us. We had to stop him. We had no choice. Mum was practically hysterical. It was like a chant.

Us or him.

Him or Us.

Us or him.

We talked and talked and talked, round and round, but those were the only words.

We'd been sitting in the dark all night. Then I looked at my watch and realised I could see the hands. The door to the extension was still closed. I couldn't face going in. Neither could Mum.

We waited and waited. I thought we must have done it. We must have! He couldn't have survived that long. Mum and I had a row. She wouldn't open the door. But I made her. She had to.

He beat us to it. The door swung open and he burst out. He collapsed on to the sofa. Mum bent over him. Sick as he was, he went for her, but he was really ill, couldn't do much. Mum tried to persuade him to go back and lie down in the extension.

He wanted a doctor. I had to stall him somehow, so I said I'd make him some hot milk to settle his stomach. That seemed to calm him down. What a good daughter Beth was and what a bad wife he had.

Mum watched him moaning and I could see her start to calm down. Then she turned on him. Told him she should have had him locked up the minute he showed his face again. Maybe he realised he was going to die, because he didn't care. He swore he'd kill us both. And Rachel! He'd got nothing to lose. He meant every word. You could see it in his face.

Only this time, he was the weak one and we were strong. He was too ill to get up. Mum got the aspirin from the cupboard. We'd have to dose his food. There were only three, so I had to go for more from the Trading Post.

It was unbelievable! Walking away from the house and into the shop. Impossible that people were living normal lives out there, while we were struggling out of hell. But no-one noticed anything wrong. I was just Beth Jordache on an errand of mercy for her mother. Poor old Mandy's got a bad headache.

Patricia Farnham even called round while we were grinding up the tablets. I told her Mum had a migraine and told Dad it was a salesman at the door. I put some milk on to warm up, so we'd have something to dissolve the aspirins in. We didn't hear Dad come up behind us.

"You bloody pair of bitches," he said. He knew at once what we were doing.

"Someone should have done it years ago," I said.

Then he hit me again and again and again. I was on the floor, my hands over my face, trying to keep him away!

Too strong.

No escape.

Him or us.

He was hitting and hitting and hitting me. He was killing me. I was blacking out. I tried to stop, I knew if I let go, I'd never wake up. My nightmares were coming true! I didn't know whether I was waking or sleeping, living or dying.

Then he stopped. Sudden. He slumped on to me. A weight on my legs. The smell of drink and vomit by my face. Sweat on my hands. I pushed and he rolled away from me. As easily as that. His face. No smile.

I looked up. Mum had a knife in her hands, the big kitchen one.

I should have been horrified. Disgusted. Frightened. My skin should have been crawling. But it was as though I'd pushed a ten ton weight from my heart when I pushed his body away.

Mum dropped the knife and we just walked away. I've had a bath – just one – and I feel perfectly clean. Mum's in there now. We're going to have to do something with him in a while.

Before that, I want to enjoy the first moments of real freedom I've ever known.

8th May 1993

I didn't have a nightmare last night. I slept right through. My head feels perfectly clear. Like when you've been ill, with flu or something, and you wake up one day, knowing you're better.

I got up and had another bath, to celebrate. Then I found colours and put them on. A red shirt. Faded blue jeans and a patterned waistcoat. I don't know how the jeans got faded. I haven't worn them for ages. Mum kept buying me colourful clothes. I kept putting them in the back of the wardrobe. Perhaps we both knew all along it was only a matter of time before I'd need them.

Mum didn't sleep properly. She's in a state. A complete wreck, shaking and not speaking above a whisper.

"What are we going to do with him? What will we tell Rachel?"

The thing that put me in control seems to have taken hers away. But I can do it. With her help.

The first step was to get him off the kitchen floor and out of sight. The extension was the obvious place for now. It was like I knew exactly what to do. As if I've been planning this all my life.

I threw a blanket over him, just in case. Which was the right thing to do, considering how many visitors we had. First, Rach came back early. She's no fool, but I managed to bundle her off to school. I wish she wasn't so used to there being things not to talk about in our house. Then Peter Harrison called round. I got rid of him too.

Sinbad called round. I told him Dad had passed out drunk. No problem. He brought it on himself.

Soon I can have a normal life, with boyfriends and parties and staying out late. But not yet.

I went round to the Trading Post to stock up. Bleach, bin bags, packing tape and air fresheners. I made up this story about the drains. It came to me without any effort. Just there, in my head when I needed it.

Mum got completely hysterical with guilt. I told her – she stabbed him in self-defence and to protect me. He was going to kill me, so she had every right to stop him. She knows it, but doesn't feel it yet. It's up to me to tell her and tell her and tell her until it's real.

I taped him up inside the bin bags. I used ten of them and two whole rolls of packing tape.

We're safe now. He can't escape. Ever! I had to get Mum to help me drag him into the extension. I couldn't believe how heavy he was.

There was nothing I couldn't do today. The endless plotting and planning were gone: if he comes back drunk, we'll hide. If he's sober, we'll pretend to smile. If he doesn't come back, we'll hold our breaths, waiting for him to dictate the next part of our lives.

That's all over now.

10th May 1993

There was blood all over the carpet tiles in the kitchen. Mum and I scrubbed for hours, but it wasn't going to shift. He's still making life as awkward as he can. In the end, we had to take them up. They're in a bin bag now, waiting to be buried.

The knife's in there, as well. It had been lying half under the cupboard where Mum had dropped it. When she spotted it, her face went grey – so grey it couldn't get any paler. Her lips were the same colour as her cheeks, like dirty snow. She crawled over to the knife and picked it up with a thumb and finger, as if she was afraid of it. It was covered in blood.

His blood.

Not ours.

We've won!

We don't have to be afraid any more.

When Rachel came back, there was just a space where the tiles had been. She wanted to know what had happened, of course. I told her Dad had come home drunk and had thrown up all over the place. It was a completely believable story. How often did he *really* do that? Rachel didn't think anything of it. Poor kid – it was just like old times!

Then I said he'd left and wasn't likely to be back. That was much harder for her to take in. She was so upset, I almost regretted what we'd done.

Only almost.

When I remembered what he'd done to her, what she's

going through, I knew I had to see it to the bitter end. We stopped him before he could corrupt her even more, but she's still left with the hurt. She hasn't learned to be angry with him yet.

Mum's being destroyed by all this. She's even started smoking again. I threw them away. I hope I can get her through this okay. Can I be strong enough for both of us?

Whoever invented air freshener was on to a good thing. The body's definitely decomposing. The drains excuse was brilliant. It's exactly what it smells like.

Then there was nearly a disaster! A policeman called round. Incredible! They've found Dad's watch. Of all the things that get stolen in this country, they have to find that. What about the people who deserve to get their stuff back? Good, nice, ordinary people, who don't beat their wives and rape their daughters.

This policeman was alright, only a bit too helpful. Everyone seems really keen to do our DIY – first Sinbad, then him. Mum and I said we hadn't seen Dad for months.

"We've no idea why he put down this house as his forwarding address, officer. He's not allowed anywhere near. Can we get you a cup of tea?"

Fatal!

We should never have let him get so cosy. Next thing we know, he's offering to unblock our drains.

"I should have been a plumber," he said, "Not a policeman."

It took all my powers of invention to keep him from going in the extension. We were both trembling for hours after he left.

We're going to have to do something about burying the

body soon, though. We can't go on treating the house as a fortress. Mike Dixon came round later, wanting to help me with my revision. The usual excuses! Did he really think I'd fall for that one? I told him I wasn't interested, but it took a lot to knock him back. The conceit of some lads!

13th May 1993

My back aches, my legs ache, my arms ache, my fingers ache. Even my hair aches. I'm never going to believe anything I see on the telly ever again. If a body needs to be buried for a murder mystery, a couple of fairly weedy lads can dig a grave during the adverts. I've been hacking away at the back garden the whole day and I've hardly made a dent. But the bath is running and I've put a whole bottle of bubbles in, so all the pain will melt away.

This pain is a luxury – it proves I'm alive. It comes because I put it there, I made my body work.

Me.

At last, I'm in control of my own life.

I've told everyone I'm making an ornamental pond. Beth the fanatical landscape gardener! Even if they think I'm a bit odd, they put it down to the pressure of A levels.

I can't believe how cold I'm being. It's like I'm on remote, not really here, as if I'm just watching what's going on. I feel like I've got loads of time to make every decision. Everything's happening in slow motion. Maybe I used up every scrap of emotion that night. There's none left. It's such a relief not to feel anything.

My revision is going really well. I might just get to Guy's Hospital yet!

I wish Mum and Rachel could feel like this. Mum's still going round like she's in shock. I have to prod and coax her into doing every little thing. There's no chance of even starting to talk about anything except the practicalities. She's totally passive, waiting for me to give the orders. I want to put my arms round her and squeeze the pressure away, but I'm afraid my wonderful feeling will be squeezed out too. One of us has to keep strong. I have to protect myself for now – for *all* our sakes.

Rachel's noticed the difference. She wanted to go out this evening, to get away from the smell. There was none of the usual inquisition. Who are you going with? Where do they live? What time will you be back? The trouble is, she blames herself for Dad leaving.

She actually said it: "He was in my room. It's my fault."

Why can't I get through to her? It's not her fault or mine or Mum's. It was his own fault. He had to go. Permanently! In a way, I'd love to be able to tell her, to get him out of her life for good. While she thinks he's alive, she'll always be hoping he'll come back.

18th May 1993

It took days to dig the grave, but it's finally done. Just as well – we'd have had the environmental health people in here if the smell had got any worse.

There's no end to the lies I've had to tell because of him. Jean Crosbie called round. I told her Dad had left after a row. Well – It's sort of true, in a way. Mrs. Crosbie was really nice and sympathetic, but Mum can't take advantage of it, in case something slips out. I've used her migraines as an excuse for why she's looking so awful. He made us tell the lies, but he also made sure they're believable. Who wouldn't look like a ghost after they way he behaved?

Sinbad got a different story – a really melodramatic one! The carpet tiles and knife were in a bin bag by the dustbin. The binmen were coming round, so I thought it was safe to leave it there for a few moments, only they didn't take it. Then this cat started scratching at the bag and tore a hole in it. The tiles started to escape, so Sinbad grabbed the bag and ran after the bin lorry. He couldn't catch up and the bag split. It was awful! All this incriminating evidence scattered over the grass.

He came round later on because he'd found the knife. We told him Dad had stabbed Mum. She was perfect – scared, but she got the story out. Of course, Sinbad believed her. He even said he thought that's what had happened.

Sinbad gave me a hand with the digging. I don't know how he can fail to put two and two together, but he hasn't. He said I was digging too deep for a pond. I gave him some rubbish about keeping the fish warm. It was a right load of nonsense, but he didn't turn a a hair. Perhaps he's a genuinely straightforward, honest man. Perhaps his mind couldn't begin to imagine what really went on. Why couldn't he have been my father? He'd have been brilliant. I can just imagine him larking about with his kids, telling pathetic jokes and being gentle when he bathed them. No one would ever be afraid of him. He said if we needed anything, he's here for us.

He meant it.

If only we could tell him the truth.

The hole sat out there, waiting, while we ate our supper

and let it get dark. I did my revision in perfect peace. Mum pretended to do some sewing, but she didn't put in more than three stitches. When Rachel was fast asleep, it was time.

The smell when we opened the extension was indescribable. It filled the room. You could almost touch it. I wanted to heave. I had to put my hanky up to my face before I could get in there. Thank God I used so many bin bags.

I had to get Mum to help me move the body to the grave. It didn't look like anything much, just a big, clumsy package. Part of me wanted to open it up, to check it was really him – and to see him rot.

It took us quarter of an hour just to drag it outside. I was sure someone was going to notice us crawling around in the dark. It was our lucky night – for once no-one was about. Rachel didn't even stir!

We got it over the edge of the hole. I persuaded Mum to go inside then. She was trembling and I was worried she would be sick. I shoved the body over the edge. There was a dull thud as it hit the bottom. It looked so harmless now.

He can never do anything to us ever again. By midnight, the garden was level again. All you can see is a patch of dirt in the lawn where I was digging.

21st May 1993

I'm okay, I think, but Mum and Rachel aren't. Exams are a great excuse. People were a bit surprised that I didn't go through with the pond, but no-one really said anything. They put it down to nerves, I suppose. Rachel was a bit fed up. She thought we could have a little pond like the one Dad built at our old house. As if we wanted anything to remind us of him here. She misses him, though. She keeps saying she wants him to come back. If only we could tell her he's dead, without saying how.

Mum isn't sleeping or eating or doing anything. She just sits in the living room worrying. I feel like I can't leave her for a moment. While I was upstairs this afternoon, revising, she was on the phone to the police. *The police.* She'd never phone them when he was beating the hell out of her, but now it's her duty as a moral citizen to report what she's done!

It's hard not to get angry, but it's not the same for her. She loved him and he destroyed her. She hasn't got my hatred to keep her going, to keep her strong. This whole business is driving us apart. I want to talk to her about it, but it hurts her too much. I can't let up for one second. I only hope she'll get over it, given time. She's here, but I miss her.

We had the policeman round again. Mum called them. She's falling to pieces in front of my eyes. Luckily, it was the same bloke who called about Dad's watch, which made it a bit easier. The would-be plumber!

Mum's call had been completely incoherent, so it was easy to make up a story. I told him Mum hadn't actually seen Dad, but that he'd made a threatening phone call. Mum was so upset, she hadn't really known what she was saying. The policeman was dead sympathetic. He said if Dad rang again, we were to get in touch straight away and they'd put an intercept on the line. I could hardly say how I knew we'd never, ever get another call!

Two minutes later, Sinbad was at the door wanting to know how Mum was – and why the police car had been outside. The best thing about our nosy neighbours is what they don't see!

Mum's really anxious about the cover ups and lies. If only she'd realise it's going to all come to an end. At long last, there's light at the end of the tunnel. It can only get easier and easier. We've already handled two visits from the police. What could be worse? It was the right thing to do. We've got our lives back.

24th May 1993

A Levels start tomorrow.

Later on today. It's 4 o'clock in the morning and I can't sleep. I'm being pathetic! How can I scrape through if I'm exhausted? I know the stuff inside out and backwards. Chemistry's first, the practical. I shouldn't mind it – it's perfectly straightforward. There's no problem.

So why can't I sleep?

Why is it starting to go wrong?

It's him.

He's out there.

Waiting for me.

No, he's not! His body's buried in the garden. There's nothing left of him. He cannot do any more harm. I'm just freaked because it's the middle of the night and I've got my A Levels. It's perfectly natural to be nervous. These are the most important exams of my life. I have to pass them to be a doctor. Concentrate on that.

All I need is sleep.

28th May 1993

We were doing fine. It was supposed to get easier. What's happening now? I keep telling myself it's the exams, but it's not. It's him. He won't leave me alone.

I'm not comfortable with the curtains open or with them closed. Open, he's got easy access. Closed and I can't see him coming. I'm aware of the window while I read. I've got to be strong for Mum and Rachel – and for myself! I've got to pass these exams well. I will not let him rule my life any longer.

But the battle isn't over, yet.

A dog tried to dig him up. Disgusting animal! A scavenger, like the cat that attacked the bin bags. I emptied a bucket of water over him and he ran off. I'm going to put repellent on the site every day.

As if all this wasn't enough, Mum got a letter from Mrs. Shackleton saying we've got to move. Since Dad's gone for good, we don't need a safe house any more. It's so ironic! We're only safe while we've got this place, while we can keep an eye on the garden.

I can just about keep up the pretence of being together in front of Mum. I've got no choice – she's been knocked sideways by the news. Not that she'd had a chance to recover in the first place! I tried to reassure her. The charity's not going to rush us, they'll have to find us somewhere else to live. In any case, I've buried him deep. There's no reason why anyone should find him even if we do have to move. Nobody cared about him, so no-one will miss him. We'll be alright.

If I say it enough to Mum, maybe I'll start believing it myself.

I wish he'd leave us alone.

9th June 1993

I can't keep away from the window. I'm getting obsessed, checking and checking that the earth hasn't been disturbed. In the dark, it's deceptiye. I haven't properly been to bed for days.

Mum hasn't really noticed. She sleeps all the time. But I dread the nightmares.

We did the right thing, it was him or us.

Am I going mad?

We did the right thing.

Him or us.

Us or him.

Him or us.

We were the victims, he deserved to be put down – so why do I feel so guilty?

Mum thinks Sinbad knows. It's not anything he's said exactly – he's been around here a lot, that's all. She feels watched. Mum asked me if I thought we could tell him the truth. I want to, but we can't trust anyone. If he did know, I'm pretty sure he'd be alright about it. I can't be certain, though. What if he went to the police? We could go to prison. It would be totally unfair. The law couldn't protect us, so we protected ourselves. We've got to go on alone. There's no choice!

12th June 1993

That's it. I've failed. There's nothing more I can do. I might as well give in and go to the police. At least then it would all stop. My life's a ruin. He's ruined it. I can't pass my exams now. I can't go to Guy's, I can't be a doctor, I can't do anything.

I got through general studies – no problem. It's like answering a quiz show or something. Nobody could fail it.

It was Chemistry part 2 this afternoon. I was really well prepared. It's ages since I did anything but revise. I'd got the equations book off by heart. If I closed my eyes, I could see the periodic table in my head.

But I just couldn't stop thinking about him.

Two o'clock came, and we were all sitting there. The desks were well apart. No copying. Lined paper in the centre, the questions face down in the right hand corner, scrap paper top left. When the teacher tells you, you can turn the questions over and begin. Wait until the exact right moment, take a breath and get going. You have three hours.

I actually like exams. The adrenalin pumps everything else out of the way. It's impossible to admit that, of course. Everyone would think I was a real creep. The chemistry paper was fine – quite difficult, but all the topics I knew best were there. Choose six out of the twelve questions. Three were easy, and I did them first. But then I couldn't concentrate, I had visions of him, what if someone found him, what if the police came round. I panicked – ran out of the exam room.

The next thing I knew, I was in my bedroom.

Mum came in and I told her what had happened. She said it'll soon be over, just one more week until the end of the exams. But it'll never be over while he's out there. If they move us from here, they'll find him. I can't stop thinking about it, it goes round and round in my head till I'm dizzy.

She held me in her arms like I was Rachel. It was like she'd woken up again. Maybe she's been getting better for days, but I've been too wrapped up in my exams to notice. It was such a relief to be able to cry. I haven't let myself do that since the practicals. Mum said I wasn't to worry. We don't have to decide anything until they move us, then she'll be the one to come up with a plan. I believed her.

She ran me a bath and made scrambled eggs for tea, like I had a cold or something! I was asleep by half past nine.

In my dream, I heard him laughing. He never did that in real life. His voice was the same, though. All it said was I'll never let you go. I saw his face. That smile.

I had to go outside. I had to make him shut up. I was in the garden, attacking the grave. I just wanted him to leave me alone . . . I didn't care about the neighbours. Let them know what he's done, what we've done.

Sinbad came out. Why was he round at our place anyway? I don't know. He put his arms round me and let me cry into his shoulder. Then he and Mum put me to bed like a little girl. They stayed until I was asleep.

14th June 1993

Sinbad had to stop me calling the police this afternoon. For a few brief moments, I was finally in control of my life, but it's gone out of the window.

I had to tell someone.
> Too many secrets.
>> Too heavy.
>>> His weight on top of me.

I couldn't cope. It wasn't logical. All I could think was that if I told someone, they'd make it stop.

Mum and Sinbad were there for me, talking calmly and logically. Taking control. Mum may be right – I think Sinbad really does know and he doesn't mind. He wasn't surprised at what I said. Perhaps I confirmed his suspicions.

It was like I screamed it out of my system. Funny how Mum finds her strength when I lose mine – just as well really.

I spent the afternoon asleep. When I woke up, Mum was waiting. I told her how angry I was with myself for running away from the chemistry exam. She said Dad had made a mess of my life for long enough. I can't let him carry on. It's what I say to myself all the time. Coming from her, I really believed it. I wish I hadn't messed up the exam, though. Mum would have been so proud of me if I'd done well.

Sinbad's such an idiot. He climbed up to my bedroom window on a ladder with my physics text book in his hand. It's Physics Part 3 tomorrow. He asked me about the force of gravity and pretended to fall off when I gave him the answer. That's one fact that'll definitely stick in my head.

I am going to do it. Even if I have failed chemistry, I can always retake it. Maybe Guy's will hold my place open for another year. There's other places, if they won't. He's dead and buried – I'm alive.

That's the best revenge of all!

18th June 1993

A levels are finally over, thank God!

Physics wasn't bad in the end – nothing about gravity, though. There was this big inquest about why I ran out of Chemistry Part 2. Actually, everyone at college was dead sympathetic, going on about having worked so well all year and what a shame one incident could have put paid to my chances. Was there any trouble at home? I nearly ruined everything by laughing, but I used more or less the same story I gave to the police. My tutor's written a note to the exam board, so I'll get the benefit of the doubt if I'm borderline. I doubt if it'll be enough for a B, which is what I need for Guy's. Still, if I scrape Bs in the other three, and manage a C in Chemistry, maybe they'll hold my place open for a year while I retake.

We're off on holiday tomorrow. Sinbad's friends lent us a caravan in Wales. Should be a good laugh!

It'll be a real chance to forget the last few months completely. I'm packing nothing but trashy novels – no classics, no text books and definitely no murder mysteries!

I'm sure Mum's right, Sinbad *does* know what's going on, if not exactly, then he's got a good idea. He's offered to extend the patio while we're gone, to cover the scar on the lawn where the pond was supposed to go. After all that panic about moving out, Mum had a letter from Mrs. Shackleton saying we've got six months' grace. A lot can happen in that time. Maybe we can find a better place to put him.

Anyway, I'm not even going to think about it for the next two weeks.

22nd July 1993 (Wales)

This holiday was just what we needed. I haven't done a thing, not even written in my diary, which is probably a good sign, since it's usually full of doom and gloom. We're going back to Liverpool tomorrow, so I thought I ought to put something down. I'm a bit sad at having to leave, but I'm looking forward to going home as well. Home. It feels like that now. The safe house really is safe. I hope Sinbad hasn't done anything too tacky out the back.

It's been great here, loads to do. Mum and I have been for a long walk every day.

She looks so much more relaxed. She's like she used to be, laid back and comfortable. You can always tell when she's really anxious, because she gets the Hoover out. Here, instead of cleaning, she walks.

Rachel's not wildly happy. Nothing on earth will persuade her to climb a hill. We got her to come out with us once, and it was the only disaster we've had. She moaned on and on about how her legs ached and how bored she was. It's very strange – at school, she's great at games. She even signed up for footie with the lads, but breathtaking views leave her cold. I hate to say it, but my sister has no taste!

She's found a little gang to go around with. Their favourite pasttime is hanging around the coffee bar on the camp site, competing to see who's having the worst time. Actually, I think she's enjoying herself. Poor old Rach can't cope with the showers though. They're not that bad. Loads of hot water and enough room to hang your towel up without soaking it.

I haven't talked to anyone much. Mum said I should. There's a couple of people my age. I told Mum it sounded like I was six and she was telling me to go out to play. The truth is, I'm not feeling sociable. There's too much I can't say. I'd rather be with Mum. The bloke in the local chippie's quite good looking. I gazed deep into his eyes when he asked me if I wanted vinegar on my chips, but there was no spark. The thought of even the tiniest holiday romance makes me want to lie down and sleep.

23rd July 1993

We're back!

Rachel's celebrating by hogging the bathroom. She's been in there for the past three hours. I had more chance of getting clean in deepest Wales.

On the up side, there's a new patio outside my window. Sinbad did a brilliant job. I can't see anything escaping from that. Even when we do have to go, there's no reason why the next people would want to change the paving stones. I wonder how long it takes for a body to rot away completely. Years and years. Thousands of years for the plastic bags, I suppose. Maybe I should have used biodegradable ones! Anyway, I feel a lot safer with that extra layer of concrete.

On the down side, Auntie Brenna's been here. It was bound to happen sooner or later. She and Dad were close. She said he wrote to her regularly while he was in prison and after he was released. Then, of course, the letters stopped and she got worried.

I've never liked her. She was on the door step about an hour after we got back. She's been nosing around for the past couple of days, apparently. Sinbad met her and she told him she wanted her visit to be a surprise, so would he please not tell us she'd been snooping. Luckily, Sinbad's got a few more brains than that and we got a bit of warning. He was here when she turned up, which she was snidey about.

Mum told her she'd thrown Dad out because he was exactly the same as before he went to prison. Of course, Auntie Brenna blamed Mum and me – especially Mum. Her darling brother could do no wrong. He was perfect, an angel, a gentle lamb. She actually said there must have been a reason for Dad hitting Mum! How could one woman say that to another? What could Mum possibly have done to deserve being treated like that? It was awful. Everything that had been smoothed away in Wales came crashing back into my mind.

I got all het up and angry, but Mum was great. She was completely calm and said she'd get in touch if we heard from Dad. There's going to be trouble, though. Auntie Brenna won't be satisfied until she's found him. She's going to the probation service. He was supposed to report in to them. Right up to the end, he was doing his turned over a new leaf, good little boy act, so they'll know exactly when he disappeared. On the other hand, they'll probably think he's done a runner. I just hope she leaves us alone after that.

5th August 1993

Somebody up there must be watching out for us. Auntie Brenna kept coming round, wanting to know where Dad was. She was just being nasty though, I don't think she actually suspects anything like the truth. As far as she's concerned, poor, innocent Trevor was thrown out into the cold by his heartless wife, who was such a bitch he had to give her a little slap now and then. She reported his disappearance to the police.

It's so far from reality, it's untrue!

Mum was dead upset. She even said Sinbad ought not to come round, because of the neighbours. I thought we'd got rid of all that. Trust Brenna to stir up trouble! It must run in the family – hers and Dad's, not mine. I take after Mum in that respect. I've got a heart and I can see what's going on under my nose. I don't go round saying women deserve to get beaten. She'd soon change her tune if it happened to her. Only she never married, never found anyone to match her perfect brother.

She made me so angry, I had to keep well out of her way. There was a real danger I'd say something we'd all regret. We've kept going this long, I'm not going to blow it now.

The police came round, but it was okay. Mum's getting used to dealing with them. Besides, they weren't going to think anything of Mum chucking him out, so he became an official missing person.

The next thing we know, they're round again saying they've got a body that might be his. It's so weird – Brenna's ended up doing us a favour. Anonymous corpses must turn up all the time. Tramps and loners, I suppose. It's a horrible thought – all those people completely isolated, totally lonely. I bet none of them deserved it.

Dad was different. If I ever thought what he did was an ordinary, everyday thing, I'd give up on the human race. Obviously, he wasn't unique. You can't turn on the telly without some expert banging on about abuse. But whenever you hear about it, everyone's in an uproar about how awful it is, so it can't be normal. Sometimes I look at the men I know and wonder if they could ever do what he did. Mike and Keith aren't exactly over endowed with brains, but they aren't cruel. Not like that.

If I'm not careful, though, I start to blame myself for what happened, but it was just bad luck that he was my father.

Mum had to go and identify this body. Sinbad and I went with her and, of course, Auntie Brenna was there. We were dreading it, knowing that it couldn't possibly be Dad. We had to go to the police station, rather than the mortuary. I thought that was a bit odd, at first, but it turned out this body was too badly decomposed to be used for identification purposes.

They kept us waiting for ages. The four of us had to squeeze on to this hard wooden bench. After an hour, I felt like a criminal. I was practically demanding to see my solicitor. Brenna didn't help. She's got this way of talking that makes me want to scream. Full of your father this and your father that. Show some respect. Worship at his feet. She nearly went mad when I said at least Mum wouldn't have to look at some corpse.

"Some corpse?" she said. "You could be talking about your own father. Some corpse?"

I thought she was going to start foaming at the mouth. As if it didn't make it a thousand times worse that it was my own father who abused me.

Mum had to go and look at some personal effects, to see if she recognised any of them as Dad's. While she was in there, Sinbad and Brenna and I didn't say a word. I knew if I opened my mouth, there would be an argument.

The police station was busy, people coming in and out all the time. I expected loads of angry suspects and sarcastic coppers, but it wasn't like that – not at the front desk, anyway. We didn't see any arrests or anything, people just sort of milled about.

When the door opened and Mum came out, I swear the place went silent. These two blokes in plain clothes followed her. They looked so serious, I thought Mum must have broken down, but it was the opposite. She'd identified the body as Dad's. She said the ring and watch found on that corpse were his!

What a star!!!

Sinbad and I were too stunned to take it in for a moment. Auntie Brenna made a complete idiot of herself, flinging herself on the floor and crying. She got hysterical. First, she wanted to go down to the mortuary to check for herself. Then, she turned on Mum. She said Mum had ruined him. That it was Mum's fault he was dead because she'd thrown him out on to the streets.

"You killed him," she screamed.

Mum nearly collapsed from the shock. I was terrified, but part of me wanted to laugh, it was so painful. All these things were bubbling up inside me with nowhere to let them out. Luckily, everyone took it for granted we'd all be upset and no-one took any notice of Auntie Brenna's actual words.

Mum didn't say a thing till we got home, she was too stunned. When she'd calmed down a bit, she told us what happened. Of course, the things weren't Dad's, but no-one else was likely to claim them, so she grabbed the chance to get us out of the nightmare. I'm so proud of her! Normally, she worries and frets about making the tiniest decisions. But this . . .

We've got to bury him officially now. Rachel had to be told. We said he was living rough and died of a heart attack. She burst into tears, of course. Mum said to me later that it'll be a good thing in the end, otherwise she'd always be wondering where he was and why he didn't come back for her. This way, she'll be able to grieve for him.

In a funny sort of way, everything fits. The father Rachel misses had nothing to do with our dad, so she'll say goodbye to an imaginary man forever. I wonder if the man at the mortuary had a family. Presumably not, since no-one's been looking for him. Perhaps he always wanted one. Perhaps now he's dead, we can give him what he never had in life, although it's a pity about the awful reputation that's going to be buried with him. I could cry for him, this unknown, lonely stranger. I've no tears for the beast under the patio.

Rachel blames me, says I chased Dad away. It hurts, but telling her the truth would hurt more. She could never understand why Mum and I had to do what we did.

Mum's worse. She really is grieving for Dad. I can only pretend, go through the motions, concentrate on some poor old tramp, who deserves my pity. While everyone else is pretending to bury Trevor Jordache, I've got to remember what's really in the box.

13th August 1993

It's over – at last!
Auntie Brenna got a headstone engraved.

TREVOR JORDACHE
HUSBAND, FATHER AND LOVING BROTHER

It's surprisingly accurate for her. He was a husband and a father – an appalling one. I suppose he was her loving brother, unless her memory's playing tricks, which wouldn't surprise me.

She was a complete pain about the whole thing. We'd decided on a cremation. It felt safer, more thorough, as if it was protection against something. Auntie Brenna had other ideas! Apparently, Dad wrote a will in one of his more depressed moments in prison. He specifically asked to be buried. Mum gave in, rather than get involved in any more fights. She was adamant about not having the body back to the house, though. That was Auntie's next brilliant thought. She'd probably have had an open casket if we'd let her.

We had her here for days. Everything was a performance and an argument. I know she was upset and grieving, but it made me sick to see it. I wanted to shovel him into the ground and get it over with. Every time she came round, we got this rubbish about how he'd supported us and worked so hard.

Auntie Brenna wanted me or Rachel to do a reading. Mum wouldn't let Rachel, so she asked if I would. I said yes for her sake, and to keep the peace.

On the day, Auntie Brenna wanted us to look as though we were mourning, so I fished some black clothes out of my wardrobe.

Quite suitable, really. He always hated me wearing black.

At the last moment, Mum nearly refused to go. She started crying and said she couldn't go through with burying a complete stranger. Sinbad made her – he said it wasn't just her she had to think about. What about his involvement? It was the first time he'd openly admitted he knows what really happened.

Mum always loved Dad and always believed she could change him. She would never have stuck that knife into him for what he was doing to her. I really think she would have let him kill her. What finally did it was that he was threatening *my* life. I looked at her collapsed on the sofa, crying into Sinbad's arms and realised what a lot I owe her. When it really mattered, she did love me more than him.

I was fine when the car came and we all drove away. Everyone was crying except me and Sinbad. All I wanted was to make it look right. The coffin didn't mean anything to me. We were all play acting.

Then I had to do my reading. I hadn't looked at it before. Church stuff doesn't usually mean a lot to me. It never seems to have anything to do with our lives, but this bit was about the father of love. The father of compassion who comforts us in our troubles.

Suddenly all the times we needed someone – anyone – to help us away from our father were there, in my head. There were tears running out of my eyes, getting in the way of the words. I couldn't stop them! I was crying, not for someone I'd lost, but for someone I should have had and never did. He stole my childhood, my trust. I felt so angry and so cheated, I couldn't go on.

I didn't finish. I half fell down the steps and everyone thought I was grief stricken. Auntie Brenna shot me this semi smile of condolence. I'd done her proud, in a way, breaking down for her brother, like a good daughter and niece should. I nearly shouted it out then – it's not him – I heard the words come out, but Sinbad got me away.

When the service was over, we had to follow the coffin to the grave. I was still shaking when I threw my handful of earth in. The hypocrisy was too much to bear. Auntie Brenna told Rachel about how her precious Trevor used to look after her when she was a little girl. It made me remember how everyone used to think he was Mr. Wonderful, Mr. Charming. That smile. They didn't have to live with him. I said as much to her and she turned on me, accusing him of tormenting him even after death. *Me* torment *him?* When he tormented us at every opportunity he got.

It was the last straw, I couldn't hold it any more. I didn't mean to, but I told Auntie Brenna what he'd done – how he raped me and Rachel. Rachel, who may never get over what happened because he made her feel guilty.

Thank goodness Mum was there. She told me to be quiet. Auntie Brenna was smug, because I got ticked off, but it wasn't that. Mum stopped me from spilling the beans!

There wasn't a proper wake or anything back at the house, just a few sandwiches. I could see Auntie Brenna winding herself up for yet another session, so I escaped for a walk. I met Peter Harrison in the Close and he invited me over for a coffee. Margaret came too.

It was such a relief, sort of back to normal. They were sorry about the funeral, but more interested in my exam results and Margaret's digs. She's moving back to the Farnham's. It's great for her, because she hates living on her own. Margaret and I agreed to go to the pictures together some time.

Peter said we should all celebrate my exams and Margaret's move. Could be commiserating on my part. I'm bound to have failed chemistry and I wouldn't lay too heavy odds on having done well in the others. It's my 18th birthday next week, as well. We could have a drink for that too.

I'll officially be an adult. I've felt like one for a very long time. Perhaps that's why I get on so well with people like Peter and Margaret. Peter's a lot older anyway and Margaret always seems grown up. She's only nineteen, but she's left school and had a proper job and been engaged and everything. They're both great to talk to – it's not that we spend our entire time solving the world's problems, but we do discuss serious things occasionally. I feel about a million miles away from people in my class at college. I look at them sometimes and think, you don't know anything yet.

19th August 1993

What an introduction to adulthood. My head's still in a whirl!

It started off brilliantly. Mum arranged this surprise birthday party down at La Luz. Peter Harrison was asked to keep me out of the way. The trouble was, he did his job a bit too well. He took me to this really nice wine bar and we were chatting away for hours. I could get used to being around him!

When he insisted we go to La Luz, I wasn't exactly over the moon about the idea, but I said I'd go for one drink. There they all were, waiting for me – Mum, Sinbad, Rachel, Margaret, Mike and Keith. We had a great time. There was champagne. Well, sparkling wine, but it was on the house.

Peter was definitely making a move. He's a bit of a hunk, dead fit, *and* he takes me seriously. I can talk to him about anything. We went outside supposedly to get away from the smoke. I told about going to university. He's a brilliant listener, he never interrupts and you can tell his mind isn't wandering.

Then I had to go and ruin it by being pathetic. He tried to kiss me.

It was so humiliating!

I wanted him to, that's why we'd really gone outside. It was my suggestion, but when his face came near mine, I panicked. I suddenly remembered I've never kissed a lad. Ever! The only person who's touched me in that kind of way is *him*. It was like an instinctive reaction, as if my body was telling me to run. I said I had to get home – I've blown it with him.

While we were outside, Sinbad had left the club. I found him at our house, digging the grave up. After what had just happened, I nearly went berserk. It was like my nightmares were coming back. Sinbad told me Auntie Brenna had been nagging Mum to give her Dad's signet ring. Seems it was some special design and a family heirloom.

When will he stop making trouble for us?

Mum tried to get one like it, but it wasn't any use, so Sinbad offered to come back during the party and get the ring off the corpse. Poor Sinbad. He couldn't go through with it. He just sat there, in the mud, and cried. It was awful. He was so ashamed of letting me see it, but couldn't stop. He said even though he knew what Dad did to us, he felt awful about what we'd done.

I told Sinbad the whole truth – what Dad really did to me and Rachel. He was shocked, really angry. It was the first time I've seen him like that. No jokes. If Dad had been alive, Sinbad would have gone for him. As it was, there was only the body.

We got the ring between us. It was a disgusting job. Luckily, we managed to work out where the hand was. We held our noses and cut a tiny bit of the bin bag. The ring came away with one quick pull, then we shovelled the earth back and replaced the patio slabs. Sinbad made a dash for the bathroom when we got inside.

I felt sick enough, but I managed not to throw up. Sometimes I feel so hard inside, it hurts. I can't let myself think of the horrible things I've done. Last night, I dug up a dead body and took a ring off its finger.

Mum should have told me what was happening. I feel unsafe again, as though some horrible surprise is going to leap out at me. We're together in this. They ought to have told me!

20th August 1993

I've done it. I've got my place at Guy's – scraped in.

Physics	A
Biology	A
General Studies	A
Chemistry	B

It's so frustrating! Why couldn't I have had a tiny bit more self control? It would have been fantastic to have got all A's. I suppose the B isn't bad, considering I didn't do half the paper.

Margaret came with me to look for the results. Just as well. I needed the support. I could hardly see the board, I was so nervous. She's really nice. I'd love us to get to be proper friends. Lots of other people would have been sarkey or defensive, particularly if they hadn't got a lot of qualifications themselves, but not Margaret. I suppose it's because she's straightforward. She was just happy for me.

I'm happy for myself.

Mum's over the moon, of course – bursting with pride and grinning away like a Cheshire cat. It's not really that marvellous – I should have got an A in Chemistry. I'm not going to let that get me down, though. It's good enough for Guy's and that's what matters.

Sinbad's nicknamed me 'Little Miss Brainbox' – could be worse. I'm in such a good mood, I'd forgive him anything. Even Rachel was pleased.

The only cloud on the horizon was dear Auntie Brenna. She came round to collect the ring. According to her, the only reason I passed was because of her darling brother. I inherited his brains apparently. He was the reason I only got a

B. The more he used to go on about how much studying I ought to do, the harder it was to do it. Sometimes I wanted to throw it all in, just to spite him, but it would have been spiting Mum and myself as well.

She accused me of lying about what he did. Mum was really angry about it and more or less threw her out. I didn't want her to get in a temper, although it's great when she sticks up for me.

The whole thing's starting to fade into the past. Despite all he could do, I'm going to be a doctor. I'm getting on with my life!

I *know* what happened.

I *know* where the blame lies.

If Auntie Brenna wants to deny it, that's up to her. She's happier with her delusions. Besides, it'll keep her well away from us. I doubt if we'll be seeing her again.

There was another reason for my being in a good mood. Peter Harrison! He stopped me in the Close and apologised for trying the come-on at my birthday. How many lads would be that considerate? It's not as if he was insistent or anything. I'd have loved to have given him a great, big kiss in the middle of the street. A real long one – to celebrate my results, naturally!

We're all going for a drink this evening – him, me, Margaret, Mike and Keith. The Gang. Who'd have thought I'd ever be part of a gang?

Mike keeps giving me these supposedly soulful looks. I suppose he thinks they're a turn on. He should look at himself in a mirror. All they do is emphasise his zits. Who needs a lad, when they can get a man?

Now that I've done it, I'm not sure I should go to Guy's. It's been my ambition ever since I can remember. I don't really know why. There's loads of other good teaching hospitals. Liverpool's one of the best universities. On the one hand, it would be a good way to leave home, sort of bit by bit. Plus, I'd be in London – centre of the universe. Supposedly!

On the other hand, I get choked at the thought of leaving Mum and Rachel. Suppose Mum had a brainstorm. Suppose she tried to phone the police again. If I wasn't here, everything could come out. She'd go to prison. Rachel would be taken into care and it would all have been for nothing. Besides, I'd really miss them, especially Mum.

I said as much to Mum. She's dead set on me going. She said I'd worked hard and deserved my place and that she and Rach will be okay. She sounded so positive, I was fairly convinced. When she's not right in front of me, though, I have my doubts.

25th August 1993

I've decided to stay in Liverpool and I'm trying desperately hard not to mind. Liverpool University say they'd be delighted to have me. A letter confirming my place will arrive any moment. It's a great university. I can always try for a house job or something at Guy's later on. The bloke I spoke to sounded really nice, and I've been to have a good look around.

Underneath it all, I'm really disappointed, but I don't see what else I can do.

This morning, Mrs. Shackleton informed us that the charity is going to build an extension to this house. They'll have to destroy the new patio. Sorry for the inconvenience. Apparently, this house is in such a good spot and in such good nick, they want to expand it so that two families can hide here.

The Jordaches are not included!

They've given us three months' notice. Only three months to stop them digging up the garden. If we're going to beat this, we've got to stick together. I've got to stay.

The surveyor came round this afternoon to look over the site. I can't believe it's happening so fast. He wasn't very complimentary about Sinbad's paving stones. Now, Sinbad and Mum have fallen out. How could anyone fall out with Sinbad? I asked Mum, but she didn't really say. Sinbad's dead fond of her – anyone can see *that*. Except Mum! She tries to keep him at arm's length, to make their relationship sort of a business one. He doesn't want that – nor does she, really. The trouble is, she feels that she can't let any man near her again.

28th August 1993

I don't think I'm in love, not yet, but I could be almost.
What a stupid sentence!
Perhaps I *am* in love. I'm certainly getting a bit peculiar.

Peter Harrison.

What more could I want? Good-looking, honest, considerate and a great sense of humour. I can talk to him about anything.

Best of all, he fancies me!

It feels totally different to being leered over by the lads. Peter's twenty-five – not too old for me, but old enough to have a bit of style. He went to Oxford University, but he doesn't boast about it.

I've been seeing quite a lot of him. At first, it was mostly with a crowd, which was fun, except Mike Dixon hasn't got over me knocking him back. Next to Peter, Mike's just a kid. Boys my own age always make me feel dead old. Peter and I seem equal. He'd fit in anywhere.

Peter's got this way of talking, even when he's messing about, that's sort of serious. Whenever we've been out with the others, we've managed to have a few quiet words. I've told him loads about me – and he hasn't run off yet. He's just dead kind and gentle. When he stood up to Dad, he didn't threaten to hit him. He just wouldn't be bullied and was prepared to go to the police, to do the right thing. What really made Dad back down was that Peter refused to be afraid of him.

I think Mum likes him as well. Not surprising! He's everything a mother would want – good job with prospects, responsible, polite. All the boring stuff.

But it *isn't* boring with him.

We kissed properly for the first time. He invited me round to his place for a quiet evening in. If it had been anyone else, I wouldn't have gone, or I'd have worn my cast iron chastity belt, but I trust Peter. I brought some cider round. It should have been wine. I felt a bit of a stupid bringing it out, but Peter was dead nice about it and just got out the glasses!

I feel like I could tell him anything. Really anything. I haven't yet – it would be too heavy at this stage. I think he'd understand, but I might scare him off. There are so many secrets. Maybe that's why I'm attracted to straightforward, honest people. I can't imagine Peter hiding a guilty secret. I told him I was staying in Liverpool to look after Mum and

Rachel. He was sympathetic, didn't try to talk me out of it, or say it wasn't my responsibility. He's great at seeing things from someone else's point of view. I got the feeling he wasn't too sorry I'd be sticking around.

I asked him about his previous girlfriends. (Am I his girl-friend? Is this official??) He didn't say much. My guess is that someone hurt him really badly and he hasn't got over it yet. I'm sure he'll tell me if it's important.

He put his arm around me and then we kissed. I didn't think it would feel so nice, warm and cosy. My arms and legs were relaxing and I was really getting into it when he pulled away. He said he didn't want to rush things.

A bloke who doesn't want to rush things!

There's not many would stop and think how far they should go. I was really touched that he thought about what *I* want.

Only about half of me wanted him to stop. The rest of me, the physical bit, would have carried on. Who knows? Maybe I'd have gone all the way, but I'm glad we didn't. It's not as if I'll never see him again. In fact, we've made a date for next Wednesday. He'll have the house to himself again. Perhaps I ought to get some condoms. I don't think I'd have the nerve, though. He's bound to have some and even if he hasn't, he'll wait. That's what's so brilliant about him.

30th August 1993

I told Mum all about Peter tonight. How much I like him – and fancy him! I thought she was winding herself up for the big condom speech, but she knows I'm perfectly aware of pregnancy and AIDS and all the rest.

She was worried about what Dad might have done to me. Could I cope after what he put me through? It was like she could read my mind, even though I've been trying not to think them.

I asked her about her first time.

It was with Dad.

Like me.

Mum said what happened between me and Dad doesn't count. It was something else, nothing to do with love. My first time hasn't happened yet.

She was in love with him. He made her feel alive and pretty and loved. And needed. From the way she was talking, I think that was the most important thing of all, the thing she never really let go of. It was true in a way. He needed her to bully, to give him a sense of importance, as though he was saying, "I matter because I have complete control over you."

Mum also said he changed over the years. I tried to remember a time when he wasn't violent, but I couldn't. It's all been blotted out by what came later. Maybe it was my fault. If I hadn't been born, maybe he wouldn't have changed.

That can't be right!

Mum said the man we killed wasn't her Trevor. He'd died years before, only Mum couldn't admit that. If I thought we'd killed a human being, I don't think I could cope.

I want my real first time to be with Peter, but supposing I can't keep Dad out of my mind? What scares me most is I might not be able to go through with it. I may never be able to make love.

2nd September 1993

Peter and I had his place to ourselves last night. We started kissing on the sofa. Every time Peter wanted to go a bit further, he stopped and sort of looked at me, asking if I wanted to go on. It was much better than if he'd used words. That would just have been embarrassing. He let it be my choice, my decision.

After a while, he put his hand under my clothes.

It felt really strange touching another body, someone else touching me. I'm not too sure I liked it. I suppose it's the kind of thing you have to get used to. I shut my eyes and smelled his aftershave. Suddenly it felt good, his arms around me. Holding me. I got quite a buzz from the thought that I was actually going to do it, have sex.

Make love!

All the time we were kissing. His hand got as far as my rib cage, then he took his mouth away. He looked me straight in the eye. It was a question. I nodded and he undid my bra. Just his hand moving up those extra few inches made my whole body tremble. It wasn't fear, exactly, though that was it a bit. Excitement mostly.

As well as all the nice things, I felt awkward, not knowing what to do. It's not as if I haven't read books or seen films. I got an A in biology, but this kind of practical was a complete unknown!

Peter seemed to know exactly how I was feeling. He took his hand off my breast to ask me if I was really sure I wanted to go through with it.

"It's OK if you don't," he said. "There can be a next time."

How can anyone manage to be so romantic and so considerate at the same time?

We went upstairs to his bedroom. It just felt like the right thing to do.

I thought it would hurt, like before. Lots of girls in my class have said it's a real disappointment, finally going all the way. My first time – my *real* first time – was magic. I can't find the words to describe it. I wanted to laugh and cry at the same time. I felt like we were dancing, yet a bit of me was still shy and embarrassed, half wanting to run away.

Afterwards, we chatted – pillow talk, I suppose. I wanted to hear about this girl who'd caused him so much grief. He wouldn't say, though. Apart from the fact that she didn't look anything like me.

I told him about Dad – how he raped me and how scared I'd been that I wouldn't be able to make love with anyone. It felt completely natural telling him. I told him everything. He just listened and held me.

3rd September 1993

I got home from Peter's on Cloud Nine and told Mum *all* about it.

Then she dropped the bombshell!

Last year, Peter Harrison was charged with rape.

Rape. Of all things!

He was found not guilty, but the girl slashed her wrists. Mum found out from one of our nosy neighbours.

How could he do this to me? Why? I trusted him and he betrayed me. I told him things I haven't told anyone else apart from Mum. It felt like I was trusting him with my life and he gave me nothing. No wonder he didn't want to talk about past girl-friends. I'll never trust anyone ever again!

I went to where he works to face him. He said he was going to tell me, but could never find the right time. It was all excuses. He tried to put his arm round me. As if I could ever want to be touched by him again.

I'm too angry and upset to write any more. I've cried until I can't cry any more. The more anger I let out, the more there seems to be inside me.

Remember the anger.

6th September 1993

Why did I have to go for the boy next door? Everywhere I go, Peter Harrison shows up, looking like a wet weekend. He was outside the Trading Post this afternoon. I only wanted a pint of milk – he wanted to explain.

What's there to explain?

He may have got off, but what about her? She's never going to be able to forget what happened. If only he'd told me, I've had enough of men. All I wanted was someone to be straight with me. Is that too much to ask?

I don't want to become a man hater, but at the moment, I don't want anything to do with the opposite sex. Is it bad luck or something I'm doing or something they are? I swear I don't know. The worst possibility is that it's me, something I'm doing to attract the lowest of the low.

Mike Dixon showed up, being unbelievably smug. He was going on about how he'd advised Peter to tell me, to do the honest thing. I soon told him where to go. As usual, he was on the make. He's the kind that'd say anything to get a girl into bed. From what I hear, he has done exactly that on more than one occasion.

I thought Peter was different. I really thought he cared for me, Beth Jordache, that he saw me as a person, not just a thing to take to bed. The worst part is that making love with him was so wonderful. I don't know if I'll ever be able to go through it again. It'll be twice as difficult as it was before.

That's not my only problem! This business about the extension is hanging over our heads, but Sinbad's had a bright idea. He's getting all the neighbours to write a letter of complaint to the Council, saying they don't want a women's refuge in Brookside Close, taking advantage of the Not In My Back Yard syndrome. Nobody cares if women are beaten to death as long as it's done quietly! There's only one way to get on in the world. Be as cynical as possible and never expect anything of anyone.

You'll still end up disappointed.

13th September 1993

Margaret's going away tomorrow. Just when I found a friend! I'll really miss her. She's been a great mate over the past couple of weeks. I needed someone to talk to about Peter Harrison. When it first happened, she was the only one who bothered to come over and apologise for not telling me. I was angry with her at first, then I realised she was in an impossible

71

position. If she *had* told me, I'd have probably gone for her for interfering. Since Peter didn't deign to tell me himself, it was best coming from Mum.

I've never had a friend before. Not a proper, best friend. There were always girls to go around with, but no-one I could get close to. When I was little, I seemed to spend my whole life being terrified that someone would find out about Dad. I always used to think it was my fault. If anyone knew, I'd get the blame. Besides, I was top of the class – the school swot. Dad would never let me go anywhere after school until I'd done my homework and my piano practice. By the time I'd finished, it was always too late to do anything.

At first, Margaret and I just talked about Peter. He'd asked her to act as a go between, to get me to speak to him. She did, because she's a friend of his, but she didn't push it, because she's a friend of mine.

Then we got bored with the subject. She told me a lot about herself. Her life history's amazing. She was engaged to a priest for a while, Derek O'Farrell. Well, an ex-priest. He gave up his vocation for her. It's unbelievably romantic. I bet a lot of men would give up everything for her. He's in Romania at the moment, doing charity work. God, what a life she's had. She's done so much. Far more than me, yet we're about the same age.

She works for Patricia Farnham, as well as living with her. Patricia and her fella, Max, are moving to Oxford for a few months and Margaret's going with them. She's promised to write.

It's not fair! No sooner do I find someone I like, then she's off. Margaret says I'll make friends at uni, but I bet there's no-one like her.

4th October 1993

Today was my first day at Liverpool University. I am officially a medical student. I've bought myself a scarf, but I won't need a stethoscope for ages yet. I've never been so confused in my life. The only thing I'm certain of is that the work load is enormous. I've got seven and a half hours of lectures every day, not including the practicals and the writing up. Then there's the reading. The book list goes on forever! How am I going to cope?

By working hard, as usual. It's done the trick so far.

The medical faculty is huge – I'll never find my way around. One of the third year's spent the day showing the freshers around. He was dead snotty, just because he's been here a couple of years. He marched us through the corridors, waving his hand at various doors.

"This is lecture room number one. The labs are down there, turn right, down two flights, through the double doors, past the laundry room and you can't miss it."

Oh, can't I!

I was too excited to concentrate properly, in any case. The student union was more helpful. They gave us maps of the buildings, showing the bar and the cafeteria in red – good sense of priorities. There's a common room as well. Apparently, it's the centre of undergraduate life. It's also very tatty. There's a bar at one end and loads of uncomfortable seats, plastic and padded, with designer splits to display the stuffing. Right in the middle is a pool table. Everything a student would hope for!

We've each got a pigeon hole. Mine was stuffed full, like all the first years'. Every society from abseiling to zoology had put in a leaflet. Then there was a note from my tutor, welcoming me to the college and cordially inviting me to a sherry party tomorrow.

Me at a sherry party!

Now, I know I'm out in the big wide world.

I didn't really get a chance to talk to anybody else in my year, apart from hello and stuff. Most of the others are living in digs or halls. One girl asked me if I wanted a coffee, but I wanted to get home and report back to Mum. She's delighted, of course. Sinbad was there as well and they sat there beaming while I went on and on.

I'm supposed to be having an early night, but I can't sleep. This is it. What I've always dreamed about. Of course, it's going to be incredibly hard work. I can do it, though. Mum popped her head round the door a minute ago to say she was proud of me.

For once in my life, I'm proud of myself.

18th October 1993

Margaret's back.

She's staying in this house, in the extension, now completely cleansed of any bad associations. Her life is unbelievably complicated. No sooner did she get to Oxford, than Patricia laid her off, made her officially redundant, so she came back to the Close to house sit for Max and Patricia. They needed someone to keep an eye on the workmen who are repairing their house.

Then they decided to get married. (Max and Patricia, *not* the workmen!) Don't ask me why! I thought they already were – very confusing.

Margaret was their bridesmaid. She looked fabulous, far prettier than the bride. Nearly everyone from round here went to the wedding. They had a marquee set up in the middle of the Close. I think the Farnhams think they're a bit above the rest of us commoners. Still, the champagne was nice. There was a loads of gossip about where the happy pair were going to spend their honeymoon.

Would it be Monte Carlo?

Jamaica?

Paris?

Florida?

No.

They decided to camp out in their very own little house, which left poor Margaret literally without a roof over her head. She was doomed to go back to her mother's. According to her, this is a fate worse than death.

Beth to the rescue! I persuaded Mum to let her stay with us. It's only for a week and if we act normally, there's nothing to worry about.

Apart from having Margaret around, it's another step to leading a normal life. That's what the extension's for – having people to stay. Mum was a bit worried at first, especially when Margaret found one of Dad's shoes, but it was okay.

It's brilliant having her here. She's been back for a while, but I've been so busy at uni, we haven't had a chance for a proper talk. I really missed her. It feels funny missing someone. I've never had a chance to get close to anyone outside the family before.

Peter Harrison doesn't count. Our brief fling was over so quickly, it hardly seems to matter now.

25th October 1993

That must have been the shortest week on record – or so it seems. Margaret's gone back across the road to house sit, and to ogle the builders, no doubt.

Having her here's been good for Mum as well. She's stopped fretting over a stranger being in the house. No-one suspects anything, because there's nothing to suspect. One shoe doesn't mean a thing. Everyone around here knew what Dad was like. They were glad for us when he went.

Margaret was a stranger for thirty seconds, maximum. She's got a knack of being friends with someone instantly. I suppose I'm a bit jealous. It takes me such a long time to get to know people. Another reason Mum likes her is because we're such mates. She's always wanted me to have a best friend, and I never have before – apart from Mum herself.

The only advantage of Marg leaving is that I get more sleep. Every night we stayed up gabbing until the small hours. It's the kind of thing students are supposed to do, but there's no chance at uni. For one thing, the lecture schedule is knackering. Medical students have it the worst. It's alright for arty types like Mike Dixon – if they have one lecture a week, they moan. As for writing an essay, you'd think they'd been told to produce a three volume literary epic from the way they go on. Medics just have to get on with it.

I haven't met anyone at uni I really want to get to know, yet, which goes to show that brains and education aren't everything – particularly education. Margaret left school with four GCSE's. But she's still ten times brighter than any student I've ever met.

The people in my year are really immature. There's loads of

parties in people's rooms. It doesn't matter if they stay up till three in the morning, because they mostly live in. I couldn't get home if I did that. One girl did say I could stay on her floor, but that was last week, and I didn't want to waste any precious time while Margaret's here.

The lads say I can stay any time. I'm supposed to be flattered by the attention, but I'm not. They're not interested in me, just my body. There's not one of them that's outgrown zits and schoolboy pranks. They'd better grow up soon, or there's going to be some very unhappy patients.

Even the girls don't seem that interested in the work. If they're not larking about in their rooms, they're drinking the night away in lousy clubs. I suppose I'm a bit disappointed. I had this vision of intense discussions going on until the early hours. Talking about things that matter.

I wonder if it would have been different if I'd gone to Guy's.

I can talk to Margaret forever. She comes across as quite shy, but she's got opinions about loads of things. I went over there this evening to lend her a CD. I meant to stay for a few minutes, then get on with my work, but we ended up chatting all night, as per usual. I told her how glad I was when Dad died. She was great about it, sympathetic and understanding. No more than I'd expect of her, but it was a relief all the same. I'd love to tell her the rest, but after Peter Harrison, I daren't take any more risks.

10th November 1993

Something weird is happening to me. I think. Ever since Margaret came back to the Close, life has seemed brighter.

That's not what's so strange. It's how I'm starting to feel about her. Is it because I've never had a best friend before?

Keith volunteered to cook for all of us chez Margaret's. Being Keith, his offering turned out to be take away pizza. Marg and I took the mickey out of him, of course.

We've got really close lately. I see her practically every day. Margaret's quite a physical person, which was hard at first. She's always giving me a hug or a peck on the cheek. I'm not used to it. Unsurprisingly, our family never went in for all that.

Now, I really like it.

I've stayed over a few nights, as well. When it got cold, we both got under her covers and chatted ourselves to sleep. It was such a brilliant feeling waking up and finding her there. It's like we're sisters. Twins, almost. I feel much closer to her than I do to Rachel.

Part of me is dead scared of getting close to anyone. I'm terrified of being betrayed or let down again. Margaret seems open and honest, but so did Peter. It's great having a best friend, but maybe I'd be better on my own.

22nd November 1993

I stayed over at Marg's yesterday. We slept in the same bed. There's nothing wrong in that. We've done it loads of times before. Lots of girls do it. Last night it felt different though. I told her about Dad raping me. She was great about it, she didn't pull away or disbelieve me or get horrified. Instead, she gave me this big hug and said I could tell her anything. It's true! She really tries to understand. Most people don't bother.

When she went to sleep, I lay there listening to her breathing.

25th November 1993

I think I might be in love!

Is there a girl in Liverpool – in the world – who hasn't said that at one time or another. The difference is – I think I'm in love with Margaret.

While I was writing that, my stomach did a leap. It looks so odd seeing it there in black and white. I want to cross it out, but I'm not going to. I've got to sort out what's going on with me. Part of me has known for weeks that something's up, but I'm frightened. Really scared.

I can't believe I'm actually writing this! Me in love with another girl? It doesn't make sense. Do I fancy her or what? Where do you draw the line between affection and sex? Marg and I hug all the time. We give each other pecks on the cheek. She's my best mate. That's what best mates do.

I just want to be with her all the time. She's dead attractive. There's nothing wrong in noticing that. Girls do. We put on posh frocks and perfume to show off to each other, not to the opposite sex.

It's always been much more flattering if another girl thinks you look great, because women notice things. If a fella says you look good, it usually means he fancies you and wants you to go to bed with him. If a girl says you've got a good body, it means you've a good body!

What it doesn't mean is that she fancies you. Except it must do sometimes. Some women *do* fancy other women, but I'm not like that. I've always gone for fellas – well, not that there's been many.

The funny thing is, despite all the confusion and muddle, I feel really happy. Whenever I'm around Margaret, everything seems to be better. How can that possibly be wrong?

28th November 1993

I shared a bed with my best friend. I want to get close to her – really close. Does that mean I'm a lesbian?

The word terrifies me. I don't really know what it means.
Lesbian
  Lesbian

LESBIAN

They say that one person in ten is gay, but I'd love to know where they're hiding. I've never met a single one. There's certainly none in Brookside Close.

It's the big joke. What do lesbians do?

I really don't know. I can't believe how ignorant I am. You'd have thought it would be easy to find out about it these days. I've always been sort of aware of it, but I don't really know what being gay means. The only thing you see on the telly is a lot of camp idiots poncing around playing hairdressers. It's one of the rules. If a man's a hairdresser, then he's gay and so limp wristed you wonder how he can hold the scissors. Either that, or he's incredibly sensitive and dying of AIDS.

You never see lesbians.

There's a lesbian and gay society at uni, but if I go there, it's like saying that's what I am. I'm not ready for that, not by a long way. All that's happened is that I want to get close to my best friend. That's not being a lesbian.

Is it?

I even looked up the word in the dictionary. There were two definitions:

1. Of or pertaining to the Island of Lesbos in the Greek Archipelago.
2. Lesbian vice, Sapphism.

Not too helpful, so I looked up Sapphism:

1. Unnatural sexual relations between women.

The definition of unnatural:

1. Not in accordance with the physical nature of persons or animals. Monstrous, abnormal.

I didn't go any further.

Monstrous.

  Abnormal.

Is that what I am? I don't feel it!

I felt such an idiot in the library, sneaking through a dictionary when I was supposed to be concentrating on physiology. The last time I did anything like that, I was about eight. I went through the whole book trying to find the rude words. Even after I read the explanations, I was still none the wiser. There was no picture in my mind of what having sex meant. I know about it now, of course, but only between men and women. When it comes to women with women, I'm worse than when I was a kid. I'm right back to square one and I haven't a clue how to get to square two!

2nd December 1993

Damn! I think Margaret fancies Keith. They've been getting very friendly lately. Not surprising, living in the same place like that. I met up with them this morning as they were leaving. Keith's at Art College and they were going there to see a picture he's got up in a student show.

I wasn't invited, even though I hinted. They made it *very* clear they didn't want me around. I hung around until they came back, so I could bump into them accidentally on purpose. They were full of putting Keith's design on to T-shirts. I offered to help, but it seems I'm surplus to requirements. They went off laughing together.

I'm trying to be cool and not go round too often, but the suspense is unbearable. When I'm not with Margaret, I feel as though I'm only half alive. I'm getting really obsessed. It can't be healthy or natural.

That word again. Natural. Jealousy's natural – or it would be if it was about Keith.

My college work is going out of the window. There's no way I can concentrate at the moment. I seem to spend my entire time waiting for her to appear in the Close, then getting the brush off.

I'm sure Marg's giving me the cold shoulder. Maybe she's guessed! She probably knows exactly what I'm going through and is totally revolted. Not that she'd say, she wouldn't do anything cruel, but perhaps she's kind of withdrawing so I get the message.

Perhaps she *does* fancy Keith.

No chance!

She's been going on for ages about how useless fellas are and how we're better off without them. Keith's not bad, but he's a bit of a jerk.

I've been roped into going to an old folks Carol Concert by Julia Brogan. I've got to accompany her on piano. She's quite sweet in her own way but can drive you up the wall – she never shuts up and is dead nosey. She's got me, Marg and Keith helping out with the Christmas Fayre mega jumble sale as well. Very exciting!

There are compensations – it'll be a laugh being on the same stall as Margaret. The piano's at her place too, so I've got a great excuse to go round to see her. Practice makes perfect, as Julia Brogan says constantly.

The reason the piano's at Marg's is really sad. It belongs to Mike Dixon's family, but his little brother's been in a car crash. Now, he's in a coma and the whole family is gutted. The last thing they need is us thumping away at Once In Royal David's City.

I went round again later, but Keith was the only one in. He told me Margaret got a letter from Derek – saying not to wait around for him, that it's all definitely over between them.

Why did she tell him first? I'm supposed to be her best mate. I wish she'd say something. Then Keith had the nerve to ask me if I thought there was a chance for him with Margaret. Typical! If a girl's split up with a fella, then she's obviously going to want another as soon as possible or her life won't be complete. I told him Margaret's off men. That is what she said, after all. I'm not sure if it's still true.

5th December 1993

She loves me.

She loves me not.

She likes me a bit.

She's not too keen.

She thinks I'm the best thing since sliced bread.

She couldn't give a damn.

I don't know what to think or what to do about it. Why can't I break my heart over a fella like everyone else? It's like there's a set way of doing things between lads and girls, a list of recognised procedures you can follow if you fancy a member of the opposite sex.

First, you hang around them all the time. I've done that bit and given everyone completely the wrong idea. Margaret actually asked me if I was the one who fancied Keith! I really wanted to tell her she couldn't be more wrong. At least, she said she definitely wasn't interested in Keith herself, but she only told me because she thought I was. There's no way I can tell her who I really fancy. The worst thing of all would be to lose my best friend. There's no point in doing that when I still don't know what my feelings are.

I'm so confused. It's there in my mind all the time. I can't eat, I can't sleep. I don't know if that's because this is the real thing or if it's because it's with the wrong person.

The Christmas Fayre was a nightmare. Julia Brogan dragged me off to help on the cake stall with some old dear, who was deaf as a post. Marg and Keith were on a clothes stall. I could see them laughing while I doled out coconut macaroons to people who kept telling me why they shouldn't eat them.

Sinbad didn't help. He was only trying to be nice, but I

could have done without being told I was playing gooseberry. That was patently obvious. Of course, he didn't know who I was playing gooseberry to. He asked me if I've got my eye on anyone. I didn't give him a straight answer, so now he thinks I'm after Keith. It's all part of the game. Only I'm playing a different game now.

7th December 1993

Sinbad really put his foot in it this time! He only went and told Keith I fancy him. The first I knew about it was when Keith asked me out. I told him where to go, but he'd definitely got the idea I was interested. For a while, I thought Margaret might have said something. Perhaps she hadn't believed me when I told her Keith wasn't the one I liked.

Then Sinbad came round and the truth came out. He actually had the nerve to ask if I was mad at him. What did he think? That I'd be over the moon to have Keith Rooney falling at my feet? I couldn't stay mad at him for long, though, he thought he was doing me a favour. He would have done, if he'd got his facts right.

He was still trying to find out who I'd got my eye on. I nearly jumped out of my skin when he said he thought it wasn't a lad. Dead right! Only Sinbad meant a man, an older fella, some college lecturer, probably married.

As if I'd do something that stupid.

As if I'm not doing something far more stupid.

Standing there on the doorstep, I made up my mind. Sinbad's never let me down yet. It's a funny thing about him. He plays the fool half the time, but there's loads more to him than meets the eye. I thought if there's anyone around here who won't be horrified, who might understand what I'm going through, it's him.

I told him, straight out – it's not a lad, or an older fella. It's a girl. God – his face! He stared at me with his mouth open. With all the unbelievable things he knows about this family, this was the one thing that shut him up. I waited for him to say something, anything, but he just stood there.

After a while, I went back upstairs and locked myself in my room. I've never felt like such a freak in my life. I'm the girl whose mother killed her father, who was raped by him and who buried him under the patio. Sinbad took all that on board, but when I told him I thought I might fancy another girl, he couldn't cope. Is it more natural to murder than to love? What are people so frightened of?

I wish I could tell Mum. We're so close – far closer than most mothers and daughters. More like sisters. Usually, I can predict how she'll react. I can talk to her, so that even she'll get annoyed, because I know what winds her up. This is different. I've never heard her say anything about gays. We've talked about sex often enough, she's great about that. I really haven't a clue whether she'll go off the deep end or accept this as part of my life. I'd give anything to be able to discuss my feelings with her, but I can't until I've sorted them out.

10th December 1993

This is crazy. One minute I'm up, the next I'm down. One kind word from Margaret and everything's alright. She ignores me, and I'm in hell. There's no middle ground, it's all or nothing.

No-one would guess what's happening to me. If they think anything at all, it's that I've fallen for some fella. Perfectly normal adolescent behaviour. Substitute 'girl' for 'fella' and it is. The trouble is, it feels like exactly the same thing. Why is it so much of a problem, just because it's two girls?

Who am I trying to kid? I know why. It's everyone else! If I was to let on how I'm feeling, I'd never hear the last of it. I can just imagine going down to La Luz with Margaret on my arm, both of us dressed to kill and dancing with each other. Not round our handbags with half an eye on the lads, but really with each other. We'd be chased out of there in no time.

I hate myself for being such a mess. Part of me knows I'm acting like a complete idiot. At least, that part is strong enough to stop me hammering on Margaret's door night and day.

I feel exactly the same way as I did about Peter Harrison, only a hundred times worse. Is that because Margaret's a girl or because I'm a hundred times more in love with her than I ever was with him?

I can't live life like this for much longer.

I'll go mad!

Keith asked Margaret out. He's desperate, that one! Why can't the lads see that we can spot it a mile off? They think we'll be so incredibly flattered by their attention, we'll fall at their feet. No wonder they get disappointed so often.

I thought Keith was a bit different, so did Margaret. He's usually quiet and fairly considerate. He did it in a nice way, I'll give him that. Normally, he lives on pizzas, but he cooked this meal for Margaret. Candles and all! She told me later she still thought it was 'just good friends' until he actually started getting all lovey dovey.

I'm beginning to think there's no such thing as a platonic friendship.

I told Margaret about Keith asking me out only the other day. I said I'd turned him down and that was why he was after her. Looking back on it, I suppose it was a bit sneaky. I think he really does like her, but Margaret will never believe that now. She was dead upset.

Later on, she said it was just as well she found out what he was like before anything happened between them. Which means she does like him – or did. There was a real possibility she might have gone out with him.

We were walking to the shops and she said something that almost made me stop in my tracks.

"Fellas," she said. "Who needs them?"

She gave me this look, a sort of smiling, we're in the plot together sort of thing. For a moment, I thought this was it and she was going to kiss me in the middle of the parade.

No chance!

Every day, all over the country, women are giving up men forever, then falling for the next one who even glances their way. I've heard Margaret say exactly the same thing loads of times herself.

I'm not sure I want to give up men. There's hardly any one around here worth fancying, but that doesn't mean I'd be left cold if some hunk turned up on the doorstep. It's a fact of life that there aren't nearly enough decent fellas to go round.

Do I have a choice? Can I choose which sex to fancy? If I tell myself I'm not going to fancy Margaret any more, will these feelings go away? I've so much to lose. I can't risk my best friend. Maybe it's a one off. Maybe with everything that's happened, I've gone off my head a bit. I'll put her completely out of my mind. *That* way, at least. She's my best friend and I love her. Like a friend and nothing more.

12th December 1993

It's useless. Pretending everything's normal is tying me up in worse knots than before. I've spent three hours trying to do a report and I haven't written a single word. To the rest of the world, I'm studying, but I'm just thinking and dreaming of *Her*. I couldn't even concentrate on physiology, my favourite subject.

My work should be worrying me. I've hardly done a stroke for weeks. If you've got a problem, you're supposed to let your tutor know. I can't see me waltzing into his office and announcing I'm in love with my best friend. He'd probably make a joke of it, or pat me on the head and say 'there there'. Perhaps I'm being unfair – he was really great when someone's Mum died. But that's like an ordinary thing. In a way it's easy to be sympathetic if someone's bereaved. People feel a bit awkward, but basically they know what they should do. But this? Is he supposed to congratulate or commiserate?

Besides, I've already told one man, which may prove to have been a bad move. Sinbad's been avoiding me. I should never have told him. He probably hates me now. I'm sure he's guessed who I've fallen for. He's probably so disgusted, he's warning Margaret off me right this very moment.

No.

Sinbad wouldn't let on, no matter what he thought of me.

Why won't he talk to me?

I'll definitely see him at the Carol Concert this afternoon. If he's not there, I'll be certain something's wrong. Not even Julia Brogan can keep my mind away from Margaret. We've practised that bloody carol so much, I could play it backwards. Her voice isn't that bad, just a bit past it's sell by date. I'm not fond of wobbly sopranos at the best of times. In a confined space, the five hundred and fifty-fifth rendition of Once In Royal David's City leaves a lot to be desired.

Margaret's going to be there. Maybe I should dedicate the song to her. Or maybe I shouldn't.

17th December 1993

Sinbad wasn't avoiding me. He joined me and Margaret as we were walking to the Carol Concert. Margaret said I looked nice. I was wearing this deep red dress – my favourite. Dead smart! I said it was in honour of the concert.

It wasn't, of course.

It was for her.

Julia sang her little heart out. Now, she's certain we're going to be picked up by a talent scout. I doubt if her bladder's up to it. She told us all about the connection between her nerves and her insides in great detail. Actually, we *did* go down well. Sinbad said one woman even had a tear rolling down her cheek! The start of my new showbiz career!

I caught Margaret's eye when the audience applauded. She was dead chuffed, kind of clapping her hands straight at me. It was like she wanted everyone to know we're mates. I stood there grinning and bowing like an idiot.

Sinbad took me aside afterwards. He was brilliant. I told him how confused I am. How terrified of people giving me a hard time if they find out. He asked if I was scared because it was another girl. I said no and in a funny way, it's true. The feelings themselves just feel right. It's all the bits round the edges that are scary. Sinbad looked me straight in the eye and said he honestly didn't think the worse of me. I couldn't find the words to tell him what a relief that was.

First of all, he said it was a crush. Amazing how people can dismiss things like that.

"You'll get over it," they say. Then they go on about how they remember their first love and how painful it was etc. etc.

Sinbad didn't do that. But he made it sound like some sort of cold, as if I should take two aspirins and call him in the morning.

Then he said maybe I should find out if this girl feels the same way. I can't bring myself to tell him it's Margaret. All those comments about playing gooseberry. I told him how frightened I am about spoiling our friendship. I could end up losing her completely. He said I might be in for a nice surprise, that this person I'm in love with might feel the same way.

Could he be right?

Was he hinting??

Does he know something I don't???

There's just a chance he could be right. It's really hard to get Margaret on her own these days. She must be the most popular person in the Close. I went round to her peace after the concert. No Keith. Brilliant, I thought. Then Mike Dixon had to spoil it all. He'd bought a CD for his sister – a Christmas present – only he wanted to tape it first. While I was trying to pour my heart out to Marg, he was lying on the sofa, with headphones on, oblivious to everything.

I got as far as telling her something was upsetting me, when David Crosbie came barging in. He's Patricia Farnham's father and is keeping an eye on the house – and Margaret. He was furious when he saw that Keith and Mike were staying and chucked all three of them out. A week before Christmas and he puts three people on to the streets! He's always so morally upright and holier than thou. It really gets up my nose.

My stomach got all churned up at the thought of Margaret disappearing back to Oldham. Then I had a brilliant idea. I asked her to stay with us. She took a bit of persuading, but that was because she was worried what my Mum would say. She's here until Christmas Eve. Her Mum's coming to pick her up then.

I made up the bed for her. It's not very comfortable, so I offered to let her have my room, but she said she was alright where she was. As I was went out, Margaret kissed me on the cheek.

"What's that for?" I asked.

"For being such a good mate," she replied.

Oh Margaret, I'd be a better mate than you could possibly imagine. If only I could to tell you.

22nd December 1993

Mum had a call from the Shackletons this afternoon. Disaster has struck. The charity's fallen on hard times and they've decided to sell 10 Brookside Close. Sorry and all that, but you'll have to find somewhere else to live. As soon as they find a buyer, that's it – we're out!

The ironic thing is, the charity thinks we're a great success.

We've made a new life for ourselves, started again. Mum's so much better, she's even been making plans to earn some money. She used to be a really good dressmaker, so she's decided to start doing it again. Sinbad put notices in every available shop window advertising her services.

The house is already on the market. People are going to come traipsing through here. I can imagine them sneering at my posters, criticising the ornaments and asking if the carpets are included. And admiring the patio . . . We're in deep trouble. Sinbad said it'll take ages before the place is sold. Knowing our luck, there'll be a cash buyer in three weeks.

Some Christmas present!

What's going to happen when the new owners start making improvements?

"My dear, that patio is such an eye sore. It'll have to go." This time, we really will have to flee the country.

Rachel's in a state. Poor kid! Sometimes I wish I was in the dark about what's been going on, but not when I see how bewildered she is. She won't even help with the Christmas decorations.

With all this going on, I'm still hooked on Margaret. She might not come back after Christmas. If we have to leave, I may never see her again anyway. I'm positive now Sinbad knows who it is. We were putting up the decorations and had the tree over. The two of us landed in a heap on the settee. In each other's arms. It was brilliant. Margaret's such a laugh – she never worries about clearing up the mess or anything. I love her sense of humour. She can always see the funny side of things. We were lying there in a tangle. I was half having a fit of the giggles, half trying to breathe in her perfume. Sinbad came in and he gave me this look. He must realise.

I've got to tell her. Soon.

23rd December 1993

Sinbad took me aside again, wanting another of his confidential chats. He must have been turning things over in his little brain. Whenever he wants to talk about something, he sidles up to it. One day he'll come to the point straightaway and we'll miss it. The trouble is I took advantage of it. I never told him the truth, because he never quite got round to asking. Until today! Maybe he hadn't quite cottoned on.

He asked if it was a teacher and I told him it was Margaret. He nearly had a fit! He said he thought I'd fallen in love with a lesbian. He was hoping that it was anybody else but Margaret.

"How come?" he said. "Margaret goes out with fellas."

How daft can you get? I didn't choose to get myself into this. I didn't wake up one morning and decide to make my already complicated life even more of a muddle!

In one way it's obvious. She's my best friend, the first one I've ever had. She listens to me, she's attractive. I love her. How that love changed from friendship to this, I haven't a clue. All I know is what my heart tells me. I just wish it would tell me in words of one syllable, so I could understand what's going on.

It was weird talking to Sinbad. We were whispering outside the bathroom. You'd have thought we were sorting out a some illicit deal, not talking about love. The trouble was, he actually said things out loud that I'd been trying not to say to myself. Like that Margaret goes out with boys. She's even been engaged – to a priest!

What difference does it make that Derek used to be a priest? Does that make him more manly?

"She likes fellas and she's your mate."

He couldn't have said it more clearly. I really thought Sinbad understood, or at least sympathised, but he's got it all wrong.

"She likes fellas and she's your mate."

Until a few weeks ago, the same was true for me. If Margaret had made a pass at me before I started fancying her, I'd have been horrified. So if I say or do anything, she may never speak to me again. On the other hand, if I've changed, she might have as well. Perhaps it's a mutual attraction. Perhaps being together and getting so close has made us feel the same way. She's probably as scared and confused as I am.

"She likes fellas and she's your mate."

Only she's told me loads of times lately what a waste of space men are. Could she have been trying to hint? All those friendly hugs and kisses and shared secrets in bed. They meant more to me. Could they have meant more to her too? The more I think about it, the more my stomach ties itself up in knots. It goes round and round in my head, till I think I'm going crazy.

Sinbad asked me if I was sure. I've never been more sure of anything in my life. Whatever this feeling is, whatever name it's got, it's there. It's the most solid thing in my life at the moment. Nothing else exists.

At this moment, I'd give anything to change. Why can't I just be normal?

He then tried to try and blame it on what happened with Dad. I told him for definite it was nothing to do with that. I sounded more convinced than I am. Inside, I know the two things aren't connected. It's not as if I didn't enjoy sex with Peter. What happened between us afterwards didn't alter that, but logically, I can see how the two could go together.

People are always trying to reduce human emotions to a formula. If your Mum hit you when you were five, you'll be a bully at ten. It doesn't work like that. It can't. It's like believing your horoscope in the papers. Everyone born under the sign of Virgo will go on a long journey today. Hope British Rail can cope.

The bottom line is that Sinbad doesn't want me to say anything to Margaret. I told him he'd changed his tune, but he said that's because he didn't realise who it was before. He also said she wouldn't want to know, which is exactly what I'm afraid of.

I'm not going to ignore his previous words of wisdom. I've got to tell her. I've got to know, one way or the other. I may be risking the best friend I've ever had or am likely to have, but I'll explode if I don't do something soon. Like he said before, I may be in for a nice surprise.

I've made up my mind. I'm going to tell her tomorrow. Christmas Eve. If not, she might disappear out of my life forever and I'll never know. That would be the biggest risk of all!

25th December 1993

Christmas Day in the workhouse. I was too stunned to write anything yesterday. Too stunned to breathe. Nothing I can do will ever, ever wipe out what happened.

I'd made up my mind to tell Margaret how I feel. It was

hanging over me all day long. I was waiting for the right moment, like I've been doing for weeks. The Christmas festivities got in the way. Everyone was in a jolly mood, except me. I had to pretend or everyone would have known something was up and there'd have been no chance of a quiet moment.

I heard Margaret on the phone, arranging what time her Mum was going to pick her up. It nearly killed me. I would have told her then and there, only Rachel came barging in. The day dragged on and on. I was dreading her leaving, but I couldn't get the words out. Every so often, Margaret would give my arm a squeeze or flash one of those special smiles that means 'you're my friend and I'm going to miss you'.

I didn't get her alone until ten minutes before her mother was due. We'd put our presents to each other under the tree. Silly, really. She was going to fish hers out to open at her Mum's. It seemed daft to wait until it was officially Christmas, when we wouldn't see each other, so we decided to swap pressies then and there.

Margaret got me a scarf. It's beautiful, exactly my taste. She loved the perfume. When she put some on her neck, it was like the whole room came to life. She put some on the end of my scarf as well. I'm wearing it now. I haven't taken it off because it still smells of her.

I would probably never have got up the courage to say anything, only we heard her Mum in the car outside. I got Margaret to wait, because I had something important to say. I told her I was in love. It was awful. She got all excited and kept interrupting and jumping to conclusions. First she thought it was a lad, then a man. In one split second, she'd got me deeply embroiled with a married bloke.

When I could get a word in edgeways, I told her I fancied

another girl. She went dead quiet. Then her voice got formal and her smile was a million miles away from me. I knew I'd screwed it up. Poor Margaret. She looked so awkward. She didn't know what to say. Am I sure? Isn't it just a crush?

In the end, she said she was glad I'd told her, but she sounded really cold and distant. I asked her if she minded, if she thought the worse of me. She told me she loved me. Just like that! She said I was her best friend and she loved me. Then she put her arms round me and we hugged. It felt wonderful, so warm and right. I put my hand up to her face, pushed her hair back, like I'd been longing to do for ages. I'm sure she didn't mind that. I'm sure she was smiling at that moment.

I thought it was alright. I told her I love her too and went to kiss her. Not on the cheek as usual, but on the lips. I've dreamed of that moment so often during the past few weeks. Our lips almost touched. Then she pulled away from me.

If I live to be a hundred, I'll never forget the look on her face. It was pure disgust, as though a slug had crawled up to her mouth.

She grabbed her suitcase, holding it in front of her for protection. What did she think I was going to do? Attack her? She couldn't get out of the door fast enough. I shouted that I was sorry, that I didn't mean it. All she said was that her Mum was waiting and she was gone.

It's over.

Finished.

I'll never see her again.

The turkey's cooked. Mum wants me downstairs to join in the fun. Sinbad's here. I could tell him, I suppose, only I hate to prove him right.

All last night, I tried to go through everything I don't like about Margaret. Trying to put myself off her. It was no use – there isn't anything I don't like. Except that she doesn't want me.

I couldn't sleep. I can't face Christmas dinner. If I try to read, the words keep slipping down the page. I'm a wreck. There's only one thing for it. I'm going to have to find Margaret again.

27th December 1993

Mum thought I'd gone mad when I said I was going to see Margaret. The stupid thing is, I'm sure she suspects something else is going on. She had that I-bet-you're-after-a-lad,-but-I'm-not-going-to-be-a-prying-mother look on her face.

I had to see Margaret, I couldn't just leave it like that. Three quarters of the way to Oldham, I changed my mind. I couldn't face her. Couldn't face the look on her face. I got off, miles from anywhere. I thought I'd get the next bus back home and write to her. Then I wouldn't have to see her tear my letter up.

I waited an hour in the freezing cold. All these pictures kept going through my mind. There was nothing I could do to keep them out. Each one was worse than the last. Like Margaret telling Keith and Mike that I'm a dyke. Or telling Mum. If she wanted to, she could hurt me so much.

I didn't know what time the buses went. There wasn't a timetable. Eventually, I got into such a panic, I was ready to run into Oldham or run away completely, so when the bus back to Liverpool came along, I ignored it. I couldn't face going to see her, but the thought of what she might do if I didn't was even worse. In the back of my mind, I knew she wasn't like that. She always used to listen. Surely she'd listen now.

By the time I got to her house, I could hardly feel my feet. When she saw it was me, she just stood there, protected by the door. I wanted to cry, I miss her so much. It's incredible that one person can mean such a lot to someone else.

I said I was freezing, but she wouldn't let me into the house. She wanted to know why I'd come. My mind went blank. All I wanted to do was reach out and hug her. I just needed her to be my mate again.

At first, she wouldn't talk. Not properly. Just polite nothings. Said it was a bit difficult to let me in, even though there was only her and her mum in the house. I felt a complete fool standing there on the doorstep, as though I was trying to sell her double glazing or something.

I knew what she was thinking and I said so. She was afraid I was going to make a pass at her, in front of her mother, if she let me in. In the middle of the street, if not. I told her I only came to talk and that I was sorry. There was nothing else to say, so I turned to go.

After what felt like forever , she came after me. I was never more thankful for anything in my life, but I couldn't let it show.

My best friend is terrified of me!

We walked through the park. At first, we were silent. I was desperate to find a way to start talking. Eventually, Margaret blurted it all out. She said I took her by surprise, especially after Peter Harrison. She didn't stop to think what was going on, she just legged it. Ever since it happened, she's been wondering how long I've been a lesbian.

It gave me a real shock when she said that. All this time I've been wondering, but when she said it there, out in the open, in the park, it felt wrong. I told her it was news to me if I was one. She said wanting to kiss women all the time made it look that way.

But I don't want to kiss women all the time.

Just her.

I'd want to kiss her if she was a bloke. There isn't anyone else, male or female. I'm not drawn to any other women, but I'm not interested in any lads either. Margaret's the only one I want.

I could hardly tell her that. I was petrified to say anything in case it scared her off again. She asked me if I fancy her. I didn't answer. What could I say? I hardly know myself. In the end, I told her whatever was going on inside me went over the edge. I can't change what happened. Then I asked her to come back and stay with us. As a friend. I promised I wouldn't leap on her in the middle of the night. The most she'd agree to was a coffee when she came back to collect her stuff.

It's not much to look forward to. She'll be there for an hour, probably with Mum around for protection. There'll be small talk, then she'll go out of my life for ever.

29th December 1994

She's been and I never even saw her. Her stuff's gone. I've managed to chase away the only person I've ever really loved. Apart from Mum and Rachel, of course. When Mum told me, I couldn't say a word. I was too shocked. I felt as if Margaret watched to check I was out of the way before she'd come. She's that scared of me.

Am I such a monster? Whenever I go out, I can almost hear the whispers.

"There goes the dyke,"

"The lezzie."

"The one who chased her best friend away by trying to seduce her."

It's ridiculous! Nobody can tell what's going on inside me. Nothing shows on my face. Mum's noticed something's up, of course. She's worried, but doesn't know what it's about. I wish I could tell her. I went through what's on telly, hoping that there'd be something serious I could put on and get her to watch with me. It might be easier to start a conversation. Nothing! Mum's not a great telly watcher anyway. She uses it as background noise when she's sewing.

Perhaps she'd understand. Perhaps I'm getting everything totally out of proportion. Sinbad said he didn't think any the worse of me, but so did Margaret. *She* wouldn't even face me over a coffee.

The worst thing is being without her. I didn't think it was possible to miss another person so much. Where am I going to find another friend like her? If I did, would the same thing happen again?

1st January 1994

Happy New Year – I don't think!

There's *nothing* good in store for me.

Mum and Sinbad dragged me to a party round the corner last night.

"You can't see the New Year in by yourself."

I wish I had. The party was a disaster – for me, at any rate. I shouldn't have bothered, I've never had such an awful time in my life. Sinbad kept going on at me about fancying someone else. He didn't say it, but I could tell he meant some fella. Snap out of it and get back to normal. That was the message. I wish I could.

Margaret was there, behaving like a complete idiot. Keith invited her and she actually accepted. He was all over her. It was disgusting – far worse than me trying to give her one little kiss.

I tried to talk to her. Not that I could exactly get her alone in that crush, but I did my best. I practised first, so I wouldn't sound snidey. I was ready to cry. Margaret could tell I was upset, but she didn't come after me. I thought she would. I spent the whole evening watching her and Keith. If it's got to be anyone, why him? It feels like such a betrayal. A couple of weeks ago she was full of how he was only after what he could get. Surely she can't think he's changed.

She's making a fool of herself. It's so obvious! I told her that, but she wouldn't listen. Keith happened to be in the right place at the right time. She doesn't like him any more now than she did before. But he's a fella, and Margaret Clemence goes out with fellas.

The more I think about it, the more I'm sure she's out to prove something. I saw the New Year in by myself – in the middle of the crowd. Watching everyone else in a circle, counting down to midnight.

Margaret and Keith were kissing away in front of everyone. Of course, everyone else was cheering them on. Nothing like a bit of romance to start the New Year! She and Keith left together. Margaret said she was going to sneak back to the

Farnhams for the night – with Keith. She admitted something might be about to start between them.

I wonder if they're there now. In bed together. Laughing at stupid Beth Jordache with her crush on another girl.

She wouldn't. Not with Keith. She was trying to shock me, to tell me to keep my distance.

I don't believe it! There's no way she'd have sex with *him*. Margaret wouldn't hop into bed with a lad, just to get back at me, or to prove something. She's far too grown up for that kind of thing.

Isn't she?

Later, p.m.

She did it. I never thought she'd stoop so low. Even worse – she got caught by Sinbad. He wouldn't tell me exactly what he saw, but there's no way he was making it up. He's got evidence from somewhere. Besides, I saw Margaret and Keith chatting on the doorstep. They ignored me.

I'm convinced she's only doing it to prove a point. Otherwise, why wouldn't she have waved or said hi or something? I'm not going to give up hope. She's using him, that's all.

Sinbad was getting confidential again. He said I should forget her. Just like that. I'd like him to tell me how. I can't switch my feelings off because they're not sensible.

I'm not going to lose Margaret as a friend. I know she still needs me. What kind of a friend is Keith going to be? He's a bit of a laugh, a bit of a clown, but if she really needs to talk to someone, it won't be him. It'll be me. Eventually, she'll see that I'm the only one who understands.

5th January 1994

I'm in hell and nobody cares, nobody notices how unhappy I am! I'm desperate for Margaret. No-one understands how I feel. Sinbad tries, but he's useless. My stomach's churned up the whole time, and so am I.

Margaret's broken my heart

College work has flown out of the window. I can't concentrate. How can anyone expect me to, when I'm feeling like this? It's not fair.

My precious family's no help. I was trying my best, really getting down to it for the first time in weeks. Rachel had her radio turned on to some mindless pop. It was drumming in my ears. How was I supposed to work with that going on? I went downstairs and turned it off for her. Immediately, she starts crying and carrying on. Mum was on her side, of course. Naturally, since she's the youngest and such a goody two shoes.

I hate it here.

I hate the work.

I hate everything.

I'm even fed up with Mum. I can't stand her anxious little eyes. There's no-one to talk to, now Margaret's not my friend. Everyone at college is dead boring.

It all came to a head at supper time. Sinbad was over, as per usual. He and Mum looking very cosy, it makes me sick. Honestly, they're pathetic. I wish they'd just admit they fancy each other and get on with it. I keep expecting to surprise them holding hands behind the fridge door.

I decided to go on a diet. I looked at myself in the mirror today. Ugh! I told Mum I didn't want any dinner, and she made this huge fuss. Then she said she'd buy me low calorie stuff, so she must think I'm too fat as well. I wonder if Margaret does.

I could be in London. If only I'd gone there, I'd be fine. I wouldn't be worrying over Margaret, because I'd have better things to think about. Instead, I had to go and play the martyr and stay here.

For nothing.

I screamed that at Mum tonight. It all came out in a rush before I could stop it – the resentment, the bitterness, the frustration. I wish I hadn't. She looked so hurt. I wanted to apologise then and there, but I couldn't. That's the trouble with words, once they're out there, you can't take them back.

All I know is that I miss her like crazy. Every moment of every day. She's managed to sort things out with David Crosbie and she's moved back into Patricia's house, but I can't get near her. It's worse than when she wasn't around at all.

I've completely messed things up. Nothing's ever going to change. But I wish I could speak to her. Just once. Just to get things sorted out.

6th January 1994

I was so desperate to speak to Margaret, I went round there. Even though it meant sacrificing my most treasured possession, I decided to give her the scarf back. It would sort of symbolise the end of our relationship.

She was so nice, I remembered exactly why I'm so fond of her. We had a proper talk and she was completely open and honest.

The good news is that she and Keith were a one night stand.

The bad news is that she definitely fancies fellas.

The good news is that she still likes me.

The bad news is that she doesn't want to lead me on.

I've never had such a confusing conversation in my life, in spite of us both trying our best. I left the scarf with her. It kind of connected us.

I'm going for a walk to clear my head. I can't think straight at the moment.

7th January 1994

I can hardly believe it. Margaret and I are friends again. I walked for hours and hours, till it got dark. No sooner did I get in the door, than Margaret was ringing the bell. She had the scarf with her. She said it was a peace offering.

We've made it up and we're mates again. It's been weeks, months, since I felt so comfortable. I still don't understand what's going on. Part of me is happy to be friends. At least I'm allowed to be near her. Part of me still wants so much more. Even though we've made up, we're still sort of formal with each other. I suppose it's always like that after a row. A lover's tiff. In a way, I feel as if we're going out with each other. I can't seem to see the line between friendship and a Relationship. Not the capital 'R' kind anybody.

I apologised to Mum for being such a pain, and we made it up. Sinbad's forgiven me too. On the surface, everything's back to normal.

Just as well – we've got other things to worry about! Two

women came over to view the house. Sinbad was brilliant. He told them about all this non-existent damp and put them off completely. We're safe for now, but there's bound to be others. Sooner or later, we're going to have to move on.

10th January 1994

My life is over.

I'm a complete failure.

Totally useless!

I don't ever, EVER want to have to go through another day like today.

My tutor summoned me to his office this afternoon. Left a note in my pigeon hole. In an envelope. That was how serious it was. As soon as I saw it, I knew I'd come to the end of the road. I'm really behind with my work. There's a huge report due last week. Everyone else has handed theirs in except me. I'm the dunce of the class. He as good as told me that. Was the work too hard for me? Am I in the right place?

I haven't been in the right place for weeks. How was I supposed to work when Margaret's been taking up every single brain cell I possess? How could I let her take over my life? Ever since I was little, I've wanted to be a doctor. I'll never do it now. School work wasn't a problem before. Uni was going really well, until today. All my life, I've worked to be at the top. Now, I'm at the bottom. I couldn't even make it to the end of the first year. I'm going to get chucked out and there's nothing I can do about it. I might as well go now and make life easy for everyone.

I'll work behind a bar or clean toilets. Why not? It's all I'm fit for. I can't believe I've just thrown away every opportunity I had. Why didn't I do the work? It would have been so easy. Why am I so unbelievably stupid?

I feel like smashing the place up, starting with myself. If only I could turn the clock back, forget Margaret and concentrate on what really matters.

Telling Mum was really hard. She was so nice about it, I felt terrible. I wish she'd told me off. I know I've let her down badly.

Mum said I was being unreasonable and expecting too much of myself. I'm not, though. What's wrong with wanting to get to the top? Aiming for second best is the surest way I know of not succeeding. In any case, I'm not even second best. More like third or fourth or fifth best.

I've been given a week's extension for the report. If I can't hand it in then, the uni will have to look seriously at my situation. In other words, I'll be out. This is my absolutely final chance. I don't know how I'm going to do it.

11th January 1994

What a difference a day makes. Yesterday, I was in the depths of despair. Today, I'm almost bouncing with hope. As usual, Margaret's at the bottom of it, proving what a good mate she is. I really, really wanted to talk to her about college and everything. A bit of me was still scared she wouldn't want to know, but I met her in the Close and it was fine.

I told her about what happened and she was brilliant. She's still got faith in me, even if I've none in myself. By the time I'd got it out of my system, I was already feeling more positive.

Margaret said I shouldn't give up and persuaded me to keep trying. Before I talked to her, I thought there was no way I could ever do this report, so I might as well not try. Now, I've got a plan to get it finished by the deadline.

She's dead practical too. She's arranged to borrow a word processor and she's going to type my report for me. It'll save so much time. All I have to do is dictate it to her. If we work every night, we could have it all done by the weekend.

I'm not going to let myself think of how wonderful it is to have an excuse to see her so much. We're just good friends, but she must like me. She's my best mate. That's why. That's what best mates do. I've got to get everything else out of my head, once and for all.

In a way, everything's back to normal. I really wanted to put my arms around her. Not because I fancy her, but because she's being dead supportive. I didn't dare at first. I'm paranoid that she'll get the wrong idea. When I told Margaret that, she gave me a big hug. It felt wonderful, like coming home.

I can work. I can sleep. I can eat. Maybe, just maybe, things are going to be alright. I hardly dare write it – I'm bound to jinx myself. From now on, I'm going to concentrate on my work. Nothing else will interfere.

12th January 1994

The report looks brilliant, dead professional. Margaret's laid it out properly, with bold type and underlines and God knows what else. You could hand in a comic and it would get a decent mark if it was done that way.

There was one bit I was really dreading. The practical report. But we managed to finish that this afternoon – apart from the diagrams and they're no problem. I said I'd treat Margaret to a drink at La Luz if we got it done. It was like old times, before I got so wound up. We were having a right laugh, giggling into our drinks and getting eyed up by the lads. For a while, I forgot about being different and fancying women. It was such a relief to be normal and ordinary. We sat there with our drinks, playing the old games of hide and seek. If I look at him, will he look at me. Trying to catch a glimpse at a boy without him noticing.

One pair were on to us. Margaret's looked like Jason Orange. Mine looked like nothing on earth. Being true to tradition, we escaped to the ladies. I thought Margaret quite liked hers, but she said she wasn't interested. I was dead pleased, though I tried not to be. It's like every time she says she doesn't fancy a fella, I can't help feeling there might be a chance for me. While they were buying us a drink, we left. It was brilliant. God knows what they thought when they got back to the table and found we'd disappeared. Serves them right.

Thanks to that little episode, we got back to Margaret's quite early. She was going on about how boring fellas are, and how they're only after One Thing. It was like there was no way she was even remotely interested in any physical contact with a member of the opposite sex.

I couldn't help getting my hopes up. I knew I shouldn't! The trouble is, trying to pretend it's enough just being friends won't work. I've still got the same feelings.

When we got back to the Farnhams, I got Margaret to let me stay the night. She put me in the spare room. I can hardly blame her, but I was really disappointed. After what happened, it's going to be a long time before she'll let me in beside her again. I couldn't help trying though. The spare room was freezing. I *did* try to get to sleep, but it was useless. I thought if we could just chat, like we used to. I'd be OK. It would have been fun, warming our feet up on each other's legs and giggling.

It seemed like I was lying there for ever. Part of me was praying that she'd come in. The house was dead quiet. I really tried to put it all out of my mind and get some sleep, but I couldn't.

In the end, I had to get up and go into her room. I only wanted to talk, but she said it wasn't a good idea for me to get in with her.

Not a good idea.

Her answer to everything.

Basically, it means no, but she thinks it's a nicer way of saying it. She should try being honest. I know what she's thinking. She's terrified I'm going to leap on her in the middle of the night. I hate that. I went back to the spare room. There wasn't anything else to do. There's no point in trying to sleep. Maybe writing this will help me get myself sorted out.

I don't know what to do. The honest truth is that I fancy Margaret. But is she ever going to feel the same way about me. I've got to try to talk to her again.

14th January 1994

Margaret didn't want to talk about it. Why should she? It was awful. We were both dead embarrassed, but I had to say something. The report's finished – the end of my excuse for being around her. Besides, keeping my feelings trapped inside isn't making them go away.

I'm getting really boring about it, going on all the time. I used to hate girls who got stuck on some fella and couldn't talk about anything else. But I'm twice as bad as any of them. I still don't know if it's my personality, or because Margaret's so special or because she's a girl.

At least she listened. That's one of the best things about her. I admitted everything. The stupid thing is that in some ways nothing's changed.

We went through everything, point by point. In so many ways, we feel the same. We're both happy when we're together and sad when we're apart, so we'd rather be in each other's company all the time. Margaret definitely thinks I'm attractive. "Dead good looking," she said. Then she said if she was a fella, she'd fancy me. She'd fancy me!

I don't know if that was the best or the worst thing she could have said. It would be so easy if we weren't the same sex. We'd know where to go, but this is the great unknown – and it's terrifying. If the only barrier between us is that Margaret won't fancy another girl on principle, I must be able to bring it down. She's usually such a tolerant person. If she wants to be with me, likes looking at me, where's the line between friends and lovers?

It seemed like the tables really had turned. Margaret offered to let me stay the night and it was *me* who said no. It was really odd, once I'd started being honest, it was easy to carry on. I told her straight out that I fancy her like I fancied Peter Harrison, that I want to kiss her like I kissed him. How could I stay in the spare room? It would have been more than flesh and blood could bear. We just stared at each other. I only just managed to stay in the room. This time, I was certain I'd ruined our friendship forever.

Then we kissed. A proper kiss. Spontaneous, loving, everything I've been dreaming about all these weeks. It was even better than my dreams. And it felt right.

I wanted her to just try it. If she didn't like it, we'd stop. But we didn't stop. It felt like it went on for ages.

I lost all words afterwards. If she was scared on Christmas Eve, I was terrified last night. It was wonderful and awful. The proof that it's not a crush, not something I'm going to grow out of. I kissed a girl. And loved it.

I really, truly might be gay.

The worst – or best – part is that I don't mind.

When I got in, I nearly told Mum all about it, only she was in a state. The women who'd looked at the house a few days ago, had come round again. Sinbad wasn't there to put them off this time. Mum said she thinks they might put an offer on the house.

I should have been worried about the patio, about him, but the first thing that went through my mind was Margaret. No sooner have I got her back, than I'm in danger of losing her again.

17th January 1994

I got the shock of my life this morning. Margaret actually came to college to find me. It was really strange seeing her there. I'm so used to seeing her at home, she looked out of place. I think she felt it, too. She's got an inferiority complex about not having loads of qualifications. As if they would make her a better person! On the other hand, she has got a point. It's the old, old story. Everyone judges you by appearances – how you look, what your job is, which qualifications you've got. Who you go out with!!!

We sat in the common room. It was better talking there, even though it was a bit public. People don't eavesdrop, not like they do at home. If you drop a word out of place in the Close, Julia Brogan is bound to pick it up and hand it out to everyone else.

I hadn't seen Margaret. Not since *The Kiss*. I thought she was avoiding me. When she turned up today, I was really sick with fright. She wanted to talk. For once, I didn't. I was too frightened about what she was going to say.

First off, she made this speech about how she's not a lesbian and the thought of kissing another woman turns her stomach. How did she think I felt when she said that? Then she said because it was me, it seemed alright. Talk about confused! It's like the blind leading the blind with us. In a way, that's really good. The relief of being able to talk to her at last was unbelievable.

We talked and talked about what it all meant. I told her I don't see what gender's got to do with it. You fall in love with a person, not their sex. I'm not sure Margaret was convinced. She kept coming back to the fact that it ought to have felt wrong, but it didn't.

What scares her the most is the label. I can hardly blame her – it worries me, too. There we were, two ordinary girls gossiping, but if we'd kissed, right there, in public, in the common room – we'd have become completely different people. Suddenly, we'd be Lesbians.

Dykes.

But I'm still the same person I always was. So is Margaret.

It was brilliant getting the whole thing into the open. Even if we're both still in a state, at least we can share what's going on. For ages, whenever the subject's come up, the conversation's ended with one or other of us avoiding the issue. This time, I really felt as if we'd talked it through. Afterwards, we chatted, like we used to. It was dead comforting. Just having a laugh. Whatever happens between us physically, our friendship's still there. It's not safe yet, but it's more secure than it has been. We were right back to being as close as we had been.

The funny thing was, the urge to touch and kiss Margaret that's been plaguing my life disappeared. Not permanently, though. Writing this, I'd love to touch her right now. We didn't actually say we'd kiss again, but it was sort of in the air.

It's definitely everyone else that's the problem for Margaret. I'm sure if it was an accepted thing, she'd be fine. Later, the guy in the pizza parlour saw us. He made some stupid comment about us being joined at the hip. Margaret was dead upset. She went bright red with embarrassment. Being me, I just told him he was being an idiot. I wish Margaret had kept her cool a bit better. It was a harmless remark. She's only going to arouse suspicions if she looks guilty.

I'm a fine one to talk, though. Mum's been in a dead funny mood lately. I was convinced it was about me. What an ego. Actually, she's worried about the house. It's like a heavy weight hanging over all our heads, waiting to drop.

19th January 1994

I don't know where I stand with Margaret. I stayed over at hers last night, and we were talking until really late. Margaret offered to let me sleep in the spare room. SPARE being the operative word! I was determined not to push things. Not after what happened before. I said goodnight to her through her bedroom door and forced my feet to walk across the hall.

I'd nearly managed to fall asleep, when Margaret came in. She actually climbed in with me. I couldn't believe it! It was all I could do not to squeeze the life out of her, cover her with kisses. The trouble with me is, I always rush things. This time, I let *her* take the lead. The worst thing would have been to scare her away again. It was like I was holding my breath for fear she'd take fright and leave.

She didn't go. She kissed me – a real kiss.

It was heaven!

Margaret made it clear she didn't want to do anything else. That was fine by me. I'm not ready to go any further yet.

The room was completely quiet, but there were fireworks going off inside my head. I thought this is it – we're a couple. A couple of girls who love each other. We fell asleep in each other's arms. It was dead romantic.

When I woke up, she'd gone. At first, I thought I'd dreamt it, but Margaret was downstairs with that awful worried look on her face. It's always two steps forward, one step back with her. We went through it all over again.

In the cold light of day, she was disgusted with what had happened. She said she'd wanted to make love to me and hated herself for it. Which made me feel about an inch high. There wasn't much I could say, so I escaped to college.

It was really ironic. I couldn't pay attention to the lecture, but as I was leaving, I overheard someone talking about the lecturer. Her name's Chris Myers and, guess what, she's gay! I looked up and caught a glimpse of her. From the back she looked perfectly normal. Normal – that word again.

When I got back to Margaret's, we had yet another agonised discussion. She told me about this teacher at her school. They called her 'Dykey Drew' and everyone hated her – because she was a lesbian. All the kids skitted her, made her cry and once, even Margaret joined in. From the way Margaret described her, she sounds like every stereotype in the book. Short hair, butch walk, men's clothes, moustache – the lot. I bet she wasn't really like that. Whether I'm gay, bisexual or straight, I'm not going to cut my hair. If my upper lip starts sprouting, I'll be in there with the wax!

Margaret said she doesn't see us as being anything like Dykey Drew. Not surprising. We're not! She's obsessed with being normal. By which she means find a fella, settle down, have kids. The works. I don't see why we have to make choices like that. Her dream of normality sound like a nightmare to me. Even if that's what she wants in the future, why can't we enjoy what's going on between us now?

21st January 1994

I love being one of a couple with Margaret. It feels right. I keep on having all these fantasies about us setting up home together. Pity we can't get married one day! Margaret hasn't said a lot. She's completely paranoid about people finding out. I think she's still really confused about her feelings for me. When we're alone together, it's brilliant. We mess about, like we used to, and chat and confide in each other. It's sort of the same and sort of different. There's this undercurrent of passion about everything we do. Margaret's a lot more relaxed with me now, in our secret world. We've even started to go past the kissing and cuddling stage. Experimenting, I suppose you could call it. Until we collapse in a fit of nervous giggles.

She's perfectly happy as long as what we do and how we feel are secret, but the mere thought of someone else knowing starts her off on the 'it's disgusting, we're perverts' track.

The problem comes whenever anyone else sneaks into our cosy little world. Mum rang the bell here and nearly caught us kissing! Margaret panicked. Her face has the amazing ability to change colour. It shows everything – white for fear, red for embarrassment and blotches for both.

I had to come back home now, though. Mum asked me, so I had no choice. This business about the house is getting her down. Margaret didn't want me to go, which was brilliant. It was another sign that we're together. I felt dead guilty about Mum. It's easier to think about other things, now Margaret and I are sorted. I couldn't help being so distracted, but maybe I could have tried harder.

Mum, Sinbad and I had a council of war about the house. It would be a complete disaster if we had to move out. We're doing our best to put these people off buying the house. The trouble is, even if we get rid of them, sooner or later, someone will buy the place. Sinbad suggested he and Mum buy the place. Then we'd all be secure forever. Mum made her usual reply. What with? Buttons?

Buttons could be the answer, in a roundabout sort of way. She's going to be starting up the dressmaking again. Sinbad earns some and he's got savings. Personally, I think it would be great if they set up together. Mum deserves another crack at life. Anyone can tell Sinbad's genuinely fond of her. I wish she'd let herself go a bit more. It's obvious she likes him, but can't bring herself to trust anyone after Dad. I hate seeing her missing out.

Sinbad said he wasn't just making the offer for Mum's sake. If anyone digs up the patio, we're all in trouble. Including him! Good point. I feel as if I should do more to help. I could leave college and try and find a job, but even if I *could* get one, it would only be a short term solution. I'd be earning peanuts. It doesn't make sense to give up doing what I've always wanted. Mum would never let me, in any case.

What else can I do? Get a part time job? I always knew relationships were a bad idea. They take up far too much time and energy. If I hadn't got behind with my work last term, I might be in a position to earn something now.

24th January 1994

I thought if me and Margaret were going out, everything would be wonderful. It is and it isn't. She and I are fine. We've created this cocoon for ourselves. A tidy, private relationship known only to ourselves, but it's not enough.

I keep coming back to the same old question. Is this a phase I'm going through or am I gay? It's driving me crazy. I hate keeping secrets, especially from Mum. It's been the story of my life.

Why do people worry about it so much? Why are they so frightened by the thought that you might love someone of the same sex? Why is Margaret so scared? I'm missing something. The fear I feel isn't of what I'm doing, but of what I'm *seen* to be doing.

There's a student advice place at uni. You can ask about anything or pick up a leaflet. No-one would know what you were going about, so I decided to give it a try. I felt like a shop lifter, hanging around until everyone's back was turned. It was ridiculous. The first time I went in, I ended up with a stack of stuff about bus timetables. I wish they'd mix the leaflets up. I should have taken a brown paper bag with me.

I walked around the whole building before I got up the nerve to try again. As I went in, this guy was refilling THAT stand. He smiled at me – I'm sure he guessed what I was coming in for. He didn't look camp or anything, although he had an earring. After a while, someone went up to him to ask a question. I grabbed one of everything and legged it. My face was as hot as if I'd run a marathon. My pulse was over 120.

They weren't as helpful as I'd hoped. Mostly they were aimed at people who have come out and just need some contacts. More than half of them were about AIDS. They should put more notices up for ordinary people. They're preaching to the converted a bit. It seems to me that gays have had to be aware of AIDS, but I know lots of straight people think it can't happen to them.

There's a few gay clubs and pubs in Liverpool. I had no idea! Most of them are for men, but there are one or two that are mixed or women only. I'd love to go to one, just to look, but there's no chance Margaret would come with me. I wouldn't have the nerve to go on my own. The most helpful thing I came across was a gay and lesbian line you can phone up. It's specifically for students. I actually dialled the first three numbers, then Rachel came in. I'll have to find a call box. I don't think I really want to talk about it over the phone, though. Suppose I got a bloke? Or some dyke that hates all men?

I hate myself for thinking like that. It's probably what everyone's going to think of me. Perhaps I'm just a one-off, an oddity, a freak. What I want is somewhere I can go to talk about it without plunging in, making a definite decision. I still don't know if I'm gay or bisexual or what.

Margaret came in while I was going through the leaflets. She's still hung up about what people think and I got really annoyed with her. She covers up what she's feeling by being flippant, but it's serious. This matters a hell of a lot to me. It does to her as well, only she won't admit it even to herself.

Mum came in and Margaret shoved all the bits leaflets under the pillow. You'd have thought we'd got hard core pornography in there or something. I'd love to tell Mum. I said as much to Margaret. You'd have thought I was going to publish it in the papers! She said we agreed to keep it secret and Mum will assume the worst if I breathed the merest hint that we weren't keeping to the straight and narrow.

Straight being the operative word!

Margaret gets some funny ideas sometimes. She doesn't understand why I need to talk to someone so desperately. I can't understand how she can virtually pretend it's not happening. She even suggested I write to a women's magazine. Give the nation a quick thrill!

I told Margaret about that lecturer – Chris Myers. I'm not allowed to talk to her either. This time the excuse was that it's all very well for lecturers to be gay, but not children's nannies. She'd have more of a point if she'd been near a child for the last hundred years.

Ignoring what's happening won't make it go away. It's all a matter of labels. Margaret's frightened of going around with a big sign on her, telling everyone she's queer. She actually used that word – QUEER. I asked her not to. It's funny how important words are. I got her to change it to gay, but queer's what she meant. To her, it means outcast and abnormal. I'm not sure what it means to me what's *normal*?

25th January 1994

I've got to talk to someone, no matter what Marg says. I wish it could be her, but she's too scared and confused at the moment. Besides, I can't talk to her about my problems *with* her *to* her. I'd hardly get an objective point of view.

If only I could talk to Mum!

Sinbad came to tea again. We had this peculiar three way conversation – me, Sinbad and Mum. I was trying to get an idea of what Mum might say if I told her I fancied women. I had all these secrets behind her back. I asked her how she thought we got the way we are. Is it nature or nurture? Mum just said it was fate. Not very helpful! It didn't give me any clue as to how she'd react if it was my fate to be gay. Sinbad could see what I was getting at. He kept trying to change the subject. I didn't want to take the hint, but I had to in the end. Mum's got too much on her mind at the moment. I can't add to her worries.

Mum and Sinbad have been discussing the house a lot. A couple of times, they've gone suddenly quiet when I've walked in on them. Something horrible's going on, if their faces are anything to go by.

It's always been the same between me and Mum. I try to protect her from the bad things in life and she tries to protect me. Neither of us does a particularly good job. We ought to be honest with each other, but old habits are too hard to break.

If I don't find someone to talk to soon, though, I'll go mad.

One of the leaflets mentioned a lesbian rights officer at uni. I could go to her, but if I say anything to anyone, it's like a betrayal of Margaret. When I told her about what Mum said, she was really uneasy and suspicious. She went right off the deep end when I mentioned this lesbian rights officer. Her argument is that we're OK as we are – in our secret world. *She* might be, but it's smothering *me*. I don't know who I am any more. I desperately need someone to help me find out.

Margaret's so vulnerable over all this. I feel responsible for her. After all, I started it. She's been through a lot, what with breaking up with Derek and not having a job and having such a rough time about the house.

I can't do it to her.

I can't just blurt everything out and leave her to take the consequences. The more I think about being gay, the less I mind if I am. It's different for Margaret – she'd hate it. Even if she did eventually decide to come out, it would take a long time. I bet she wouldn't do it at all while she's living here. I'm sure people at university will be a lot more sympathetic in general than the folk round here.

On the other hand, Sinbad was okay about it. He didn't think it was disgusting or revolting or whatever. All he was worried about was how difficult it would make my life. That's understandable, to say the least. I need to find someone really discreet. Someone who won't go blabbing their mouth off. Preferably someone who's never heard of Brookside Close.

26th January 1994

I tried to go to a lesbian meeting. It wasn't anything heavy – just a get-together. I managed to get one toe through the door before I bottled out. I was furious with myself. It's not such a big deal, so why am I being so feeble about it? From the quick glimpse I managed to get, the room wasn't full of moustaches and tattoos. I'm sure I even recognised one of the women there. Not that I gave myself time to get a proper look.

Chris Myers was my last resort. I hung around after the lecture, pretending I wanted to discuss the work. I thought she'd be approachable. I've heard she is. She never patronises us humble students. Being gay herself, she ought to be sympathetic to someone like me.

I'm not the only one who thought that!

At first, she politely brushed me off, told me to talk to someone from the gay and lesbian group. Eventually, she let me tag along with her to the pub. She had five spare minutes before meeting a friend. It still took me ages to spit it out. One of the problems about being openly gay is that all the students poking their noses out of the closet flock to her. Students like me! Is that what I'm doing? I should have been put off by her saying that, but it was quite comforting. It certainly made me feel less like a freak.

Once I'd started, I couldn't stop. I told her about Margaret and everything – apart from Dad. That would have been too much, but I did say there were reasons why my feelings might just be a reaction to problems in my life. It would make sense for me to become a man hater in a funny kind of way. Chris' attitude was very relaxed. She didn't see it mattered how I got to this stage. Go with the flow, she said. Let things happen.

Listening to her, it seems so easy. I told her how worried I am about Mum's reaction. Then I got a real shock! Chris pointed out that other women in the pub had mothers and they managed to weather the storm.

I hadn't even noticed we were in a GAY pub!!!

It was completely normal, except that most of the customers were women and they had no trouble getting served. I must have looked such a fool, staring like that. Chris just laughed. It wasn't a bit how I imagined.

Now I come to think about it, I had this vision of a dark cellar of a place, full of women having fights, drinking pints and smoking cigars. Probably with tattoos on their arms. Somewhere I got the idea that lesbians really want to be men. Once I worked out that was what I'd been thinking, it was obvious I'd got it wrong. No wonder I didn't want to belong to a group like that. I don't want to be a man. I don't hate them either.

I wouldn't mind being like Chris, though. She has a way of getting straight to the heart of the matter. Her lectures are like that too. Very clear and direct. There's an honesty about her. I'd trust her with my life. She's dead attractive, too. She's dead young to be teaching in a university.

She's great. Why didn't I go to her before? We talked about Margaret getting hurt. She said that anyone who can survive an affair with a priest ought to be able to cope with me. She's right! One of the things I used to admire most about Margaret is how tough she is. It's only lately that I've been treating her with kid gloves.

Chris also said that any friends worth having will still be here for me, whatever. I'm not so sure about that!

We had to stop chatting when Chris' girlfriend arrived. They gave each other a peck on the cheek to say hello. It was so ordinary. They could have been a married couple. You can always spot a couple, even if they're not snogging in public or being outrageous or anything. It's the way they sit together and carry on conversations that started at breakfast.

Why can't Margaret and I be like that?

28th January 1994

Chris said she went to that pub because she felt comfortable in there. I did too. Even when I realised what kind of pub it was. It was odd seeing women with women. I can't put my finger on why it was different to somewhere like La Luz. Girls sit with their mates in nightclubs, but they've always got one eye out for the lads. In fact, it's one of the most annoying things about going around with Margaret. Every time we go to a pub for a quiet chat, a pair of fellas is bound to come over and chat us up. Like our lives aren't complete without them. I remember one time, ages ago, when these two prize idiots were pestering us. Margaret told them we weren't interested. We just wanted to talk to each other.

"Oh," said the spotty one. "We've got a pair of lezzies here."

Margaret stormed out. She was furious, but embarrassed as well. They were so stupid. Even if we'd been desperate for it, we wouldn't have given them the time of day.

I wish I could get Margaret to go out with me properly. This business of keeping our relationship a big secret isn't romantic. It's depressing! Why should we be ashamed of what we're doing? We should have the courage of our convictions. It would be pretty stupid to start snogging in the street, but why hide our feelings? Normal couples don't have to.

I love Margaret. I want to shout it to the whole world. To be realistic, that's asking for trouble. Chris doesn't go around telling everyone.

"Hi, I'm Chris Myers and I'm a lesbian!"

She doesn't hide it either. It's part of her, but not the be all and end all of her existence. At the moment, my sexuality is the most important thing in my life, probably because it's such a hassle. I'm still not sure. In a way, I'd love to come out properly. It would be such a relief to know what I am. Any label would be better than this horrible muddle.

Maybe I should put an announcement in the paper or something. It's a pity there isn't a special ceremony, like a marriage or a christening.

If I do come out, what happens if Margaret and I break up? Will I find another woman to fancy? Or will I go back to men?

I STILL DON'T KNOW HOW I FEEL!

You hear stories of men who come out after years of being married. Some of them have kids and everything. Imagine having sex with someone you don't fancy, week after week. Imagine finding out that the husband you've been living with for years has a completely hidden personality.

I've got to be honest, whatever the consequences. The one thing I can't cope with is another secret. If only I could get Margaret to see how easy it could be. It needn't be anything big. Perhaps I could get her to come to that pub with me. She wouldn't put her foot in the door if she knew it was a gay place, but you'd never guess from the outside. It's not like going to a gay rights meeting. It's just a pub where lesbians can have a bit of peace and quiet and be themselves. There's nothing to shock her. She'd be alright once she was inside.

29th January 1994

That must count as one of my worst ideas ever! It was easy enough to get Margaret to the pub. We got our drinks and sat down. She even said it was a nice place.

Maybe I tried to do too much at once – rushing things again. I told her I'd confided in Chris about our relationship. Margaret hit the roof, called me every name under the sun. It was like I'd betrayed her, betrayed her precious secret. How could I do it to her?

The more I look back on it, the more angry I get. She's completely unreasonable! Does she expect me to sit quietly in a dark corner, denying the most basic things about myself? How could she do it to me? I wanted to scream back at her, but I felt so guilty, I couldn't say a word.

Being Margaret, all this was going on in hisses and whispers. Then she realised what kind of a place we were in. That horrible look came over her face. The same as on Christmas Eve. Disgust. Revulsion. I tried to explain, but she grabbed her bag and dashed out.

I've never felt so humiliated in my life. It doesn't seem to matter what I do, I screw it up. Sometimes I feel completely hopeless. What's the point of carrying on? I might as well live a life of celibacy. At least that way you don't get hurt.

2nd February 1994

I decided I could do without Margaret. I held out for three whole days. That'll show her, I thought. She's not indispensable.

Chris Myers helped. I haven't had the chance of another real talk with her, but whenever we pass in the corridor, she smiles and says hi. She treats me as a bit more interesting than your average student. I love her lectures. Work's going really well because of them. She's brilliant at explaining things.

I wish emotions were as straightforward as anatomy, though. With physical things, it's a question of this goes here, so that goes there.

Who did I think I was kidding? Margaret's still the centre of my universe. Half my mind is at her house, wondering what she's doing, what she's thinking. I wanted her to come over and apologise. It's always me doing the chasing.

The truth is, I love her more than she loves me. What's more, she doesn't *want* to love me. She'd be glad of an excuse to get shot of the whole thing.

I gave in and went over there this afternoon to beg for forgiveness. At first, I didn't really mean it. I mean I was sorry for upsetting her, but not sorry I'd taken her to the pub. I refuse to apologise for feeling the way I do! When I finally got Margaret to talk, though, I saw what was wrong. I shouldn't spring things on her like that. No wonder she overreacted.

I keep forgetting it's not the same for her. In some ways, we live in two completely opposite worlds. Until she can find another job, she's stuck in the house all day. She's quite good about not watching the telly the whole time, but it must get really lonely for her sometimes. So all she sees is programmes and adverts full of so-called normal people leading so-called normal lives. When do you ever see a gay person on a quiz show?

Being a student's different. You're almost encouraged to be unusual. Maybe that's what all this is! I suppose it's part of growing up and experimenting. There's all sorts of groups you can belong to. Even if Margaret had wanted to talk to someone about what she's going through, it would be difficult to know where she could go. There's help lines and advice centres in the city, but no-one nearby. Sometimes I think the problem's not even that people will be disgusted. It's that they won't even begin to understand.

Margaret's forgiven me. I have to go so slowly and be so careful. She's likely to disappear off into the hills at any moment. I told Chris she was tough, but right now I'm almost afraid to touch her for fear she'll snap in two. We talked and talked, but I'm not sure if we got anywhere. I'm still confused about how to act.

Part of me wants to do something dramatic. It's a bit like getting your ears pierced in three places to annoy your Mum. Sort of "I'll show them". Only this is too serious to play at. The last thing I want to do is to say I'm a lesbian to get back at male chauvinist pigs. That would be idiotic. Playing right into their hands too. I've heard the arguments.

"All she needs is a good seeing to."

The romantics are just as bad: "She hasn't found the right man yet."

The message is the same – lesbians don't really fancy women, they just can't get men. They have to take what they can get. It certainly isn't true of me. I've never had any trouble attracting guys, nor has Margaret, and Chris would have them flocking round her if she wanted.

Besides, I'm still not sure it's anyone except Margaret. If I announce I'm gay, I'd have to give up men. I'm not convinced I want to do that.

Chris has invited us both to her birthday party. She'll be

thirty. She said she's got lots of straight friends, so Margaret won't feel too awkward. Half the time, I think she's laughing at me, but in a nice way. I really want to go. I don't think she's asked any other students. If Margaret refuses, I'll just have to go by myself.

5th February 1994

I knew there was something going on at home behind my back. We had a visitor yesterday afternoon. His name's Roy Williams and he was Dad's cell mate. He's been here before, only Mum and Sinbad didn't see fit to tell me. God knows what he's doing here. He said he wanted to see Dad, but there's more to it than that. He's a real creep. Everything he says has a double meaning.

Mum had that frightened look on her face. It made me sick to see it again. I thought we'd done with all that. We told Roy that Dad's dead and tried very hard not to look towards the patio. I'm not sure if he believed us. I have a feeling he's after something.

We got rid of him, but he broke in next door. It's been empty for months. It's up for sale, but hardly anyone's been round. If this Roy turns it into a squat, it'll be on the market forever. Who's going to buy a place with its very own squatter?

Dad keeps coming back to haunt us. What's going to happen when we have to leave? We'll have to do a moonlight flit, change our names and move to the other side of the country to be safe.

7th February 1994

I'm determined not to let Dad rule my life any longer. This Roy might be next door, but he's not going to worry me. Mum's still anxious. The people who came to see our house before are seriously interested. They could put an offer in soon. Sinbad and Mum are trying to scrape the money together to beat them to it. They went round all the banks and building societies, but no-one will touch them with a barge pole. I suppose it's not surprising really. Neither of them has what you'd call a good steady job.

I refuse to worry until it happens. I'm so fed up of being under a cloud the whole time. These people may never buy the house. The deal could easily fall through. Why waste time worrying?

I managed to persuade Margaret to come to Chris' party with me. It was a bit daunting at first. Not like the usual student thing – cheap booze, soggy crisps and taking it in turns to throw up in the toilet. People brought bottles with classy labels on. Instead of hiding them behind the lemonade, Chris opened them right away.

Margaret and I gave her a box of chocolates. I wanted to get Chris something a bit more personal. To say thanks for being there when I needed someone, but I don't have any idea what kind of thing she goes for.

Her flat's full of books. Not all of them were high brow. Her stereo system's something else. I've never seen so many CDs in one place before. Loads of classical stuff and jazz and quite a bit of modern stuff. If I wanted to sum Chris up in one word, it'd be classy. But properly classy – everything she does is just right. You'd think she could be a bit of a snob, but I reckon it comes naturally.

The party was going really well, until Chris' girlfriend, Helen, showed up. Not that there was a major row or anything – they're far too cool for that. I spotted them arguing in the hallway. Then Helen left. I don't know what it was about and I could hardly ask. Chris looked gutted. From what she'd said earlier, they've been living together for quite a long time. I wonder if this means it's over.

There were quite a few people from the medical department. Most of them I'd seen but not spoken too. Chris introduced me. I felt dead nervous but they were really interesting. We were talking about all sorts of things – current affairs, animal rights, how the university is run, what we should do about cut backs. Made a change from my friend fancies your friend and when did you last go to a pop concert. The music was loud enough to dance to, but quiet enough so you could talk as well.

At first, Margaret seemed to be having a good time. She was quite relieved at how ordinary everybody was. I hadn't led her into a den of iniquity after all. Trouble was, once I got caught up in discussing genetics, I sort of forgot about her. I didn't mean to. I feel really awful about it now. Time passed so quickly, I genuinely didn't notice how out of it she was. Then I caught a glimpse of her standing in a corner clutching a drink for protection. When I went over to her, she was in a right mood. She said it was obvious that Chris fancies me and dragged me away on purpose.

This is really stupid because:

A) it's not Chris' style

   and

B) she's hardly noticed me.

I'm just the funny little first year, who she takes pity on

because she's having a hard time. Trouble is, while I was telling Margaret she had no reason to be jealous, I caught Chris' eye. She only winked at me! It could be matey, but it could have been something else.

I think I might be quite pleased if it was, in a way.

9th February 1994

Margaret came to find me in the common room at uni again. She's feeling insecure about US. It's so weird. One minute she's going on about how she's not a lesbian, never has been and never will be. The next, she's jealous of another woman.

I suppose I should be glad she's accepted our relationship. Except she hasn't. She still won't come with me to a gay bar. There has to be a two foot gap between us when we're walking down the street. She's so remote in public, people are beginning to think we aren't even friends any more. I suppose I kind of gave her the brush off when she turned up at uni. It was a bit mean. She only wanted a coffee and a chat.

We made a date to go bowling. Chris overheard us and said she hadn't been bowling for ages. I can take a hint, so I asked her along. She's a great laugh, even though she's a lecturer. There's nothing them-and-us-ish about her. Margaret was dead put out. I said I'd stay the night with her. I really like Chris, but there's no-one for me except Margaret. I wish I could convince *her* of that.

I really liked having Chris along. Margaret would like her too, if only she didn't have this thing about Chris fancying me. Chris and I are just getting to be friends. The reason she wanted to come with us tonight was that she and Helen have split up. Basically, she wanted some company.

She asked us to an open lecture tomorrow. I said I'd go. It's about the ethics of euthanasia. The speakers should be really good. Margaret wasn't so keen – because it was Chris who mentioned it.

Margaret and I had a row when we got back to her place. About Chris! It was so stupid. Even if there was something between us, Margaret's got no right to be jealous. After all, she won't even hold my hand in a pub. It's like our relationship doesn't exist outside the bedroom door. There's not much going on behind it, either. I'd love to experiment a bit more, but Margaret's got her rules and she's sticking to them. One of the rules being don't get too friendly with Chris.

12th February 1994

I wish Mum wouldn't keep things from me. We've got to move much sooner than I thought. Someone's put an offer in for the house. They've been round while I wasn't here. I can't turn my back for a minute.

Mum's in an absolute panic. There's something incredibly wrong and I can't find out what it is. The possibility of someone digging up the patio is bad enough, but Mum keeps on half saying things about Roy Williams. I don't know what's going on!

That's not the only bad news. Mike Dixon's brother, the one who was in a coma, has died. Sinbad's really upset. He was helping organise a collection to take him to Lourdes or America to find a cure. He was in a P.V.S. – a persistent vegetative state. No chance he would ever recover, but hope springs eternal.

There's a lot of things in this world that would be helped with money, but nothing could be done it seems, for Tony Dixon. I suppose people have to feel they're doing something. Being helpless is the worst thing in the world.

We went to the lecture the other night. Margaret enjoyed it much more than she thought she would. She's got this thing now about not being well qualified. The latest is she wants to go back to college to educate herself. I told her over and over again that it's her I like. She's fine the way she is – much more alive and interesting than the normal bunch of students. They'd bore her silly, like they do me. She's got common sense, which is something most students haven't.

Chris didn't show up for the lecture itself. I was surprised and Margaret was pleased. She turned up afterwards, dead upset. She'd seen Helen and they'd had *another* row. We were going for a drink and Chris asked if she could come too. I could hardly say no, though Margaret wasn't best pleased. I promised her we wouldn't stay long.

While Margaret was getting the drinks in, Chris told me about the problems she's been having with Helen. I was flattered, but a bit uncomfortable. If Helen was called Jim or Tom, I'd be fine. Only we're talking about girls with girls. Women with women, in Chris' case. I was telling her about my problems with Margaret. She understood totally. She's the only one I can talk to about the way I feel. Her face went red when I said that.

14th February 1994

I'm still shaking after today's events. Talk about things coming up out of the blue. One minute I thought all I had to worry about was will she send me a Valentine. The next, my entire life almost blew up in my face.

Margaret sent me a card and phoned to invite me round to dinner. No sooner had I put the phone down, when Mum burst in and announces that we're leaving.

Today.

This afternoon.

On the 4:45 from Lime Street.

Nothing, but nothing, was going to change her mind. There was no getting any sense out of her. As soon as my feet would let me, I dashed round to find Sinbad.

Between the two of them, they told me the story. I don't know which is the more crazy. What happened or the fact that I'm left to find out like this. It's Dad again. He refuses to rot quietly. That cell mate of his, Roy Williams, has been around much more often than I knew. He claimed Dad owed him money. Like a fool, Mum gave in. Only the more she gave him, the more he wanted. In the end, Mum took the money from the collection for Tony Dixon. Now, Tony's died and his Dad, Mr. Dixon, wants the money!

This, on top of the house being sold, was too much for Mum. The only thing she could think of was to do a runner. I refused to go to begin with. It was so unfair. Mum was in such a state, she couldn't listen to reason. It was the most stupid idea I'd ever heard. What sort of life would we have? Never knowing if the police were on our trail. Always worrying about someone digging up the patio. But what choice did I have? I didn't get the chance to make any decision. I could hardly let Mum and Rachel go without me. I was furious.

We packed a couple of bags and left. Just like that! Poor Rachel didn't know what hit her. If it was unfair on me, it was twice as bad for her. She doesn't know a quarter of what's been going on.

We got on the train and as it was about to pull out, who should come running up the platform but Sinbad. He was shouting something at us, which we couldn't hear. He's not exactly an Olympic sprinter. Mum said to ignore him. She was trying to hide the fact that she was crying.

Sinbad leapt on to the train, flinging his arms about, shouting something about it's OK and everything's alright. Mum sat there, gob-smacked, so he got our bags and chucked them on to the platform. I jumped off. No danger of me disappearing off to London if I didn't have to! Sinbad bundled Mum and Rachel through the door and the train went without us.

What Sinbad had been trying to tell us was that the people who were going to buy number 10 have decided to go for next door instead.

Sinbad was great, and persuaded Mum that the best thing would be to come back home, somehow they can face all the problems. Thank God for Sinbad.

The biggest problem is how to get the money together that Roy Williams took. We talked about that when we got home. Mum's doing quite well with the dressmaking and Sinbad's got his bits and pieces. Somehow they'll manage – but how?

With all this going on, I completely forgot about dinner with Margaret. By the time we'd finished, it was too late to ring her. I'll have to try tomorrow. God knows what I'm going to say.

18th February 1994

Margaret's being completely unreasonable. I tried to apologise, but she wouldn't listen. Sinbad didn't help though it wasn't really his fault. She asked him if he knew where I was and he said out with a friend. Margaret assumed it was Chris. Nothing I can say will change her mind. She's also seen Derek, he came back from Bosnia for Tony Dixon's funeral. She said that Derek had asked if she wanted to try again. I don't believe her. I don't *want* to believe her.

I wish I *had* been wirh Chris. The more I get to know her, the more I like her. We bumped into each other in the corridor and she asked me for a coffee in her office. She doesn't treat all undergraduates like that. We talked about relationships. What else? Helen's left Chris for good. It was mutual. I'd have thought Chris would have been easy to get on with. She's got the knack of seeing the other person's point of view, dead tolerant. So long as you're not trying to put women down or destroy the NHS. Both causes dear to my heart as well. Chris makes me think. I suppose, being a lecturer, that's her job, but it's getting personal.

We'd been chatting for quite a long time, then she came out with something that sort of surprised me and sort of didn't.

"In another life, perhaps, there wouldn't have been a Margaret and a Helen," she said.

I went all stupid and tongue-tied. It seems Margaret was right – she *does* fancy me! I muttered something feeble about having to go, and Chris said she didn't mean to come on strong and embarrass me. I wasn't embarrassed exactly – more like taken aback. It's a real compliment. Chris invited me over for supper, but like a fool, I got cold feet and made an excuse to get home.

I wish I hadn't. I'm as bad as Margaret, getting scared off like that. The more I think about it, the more I wish I'd gone. Chris is dead attractive.

Do I fancy her? It seems weird to ask that question, but I really don't know. It's one thing to have a vague fling with a girl, who swears she's straight deep down. Part of me always thought it could be no more than a crush. A phase I'm going through. Wanting to get close to a grown woman, a lesbian, who's been out of the closet for years, is something totally different.

23rd February 1994

The Farnhams are back and Margaret's staying with them. They're a nice couple. They even forgave Margaret for squatting and told Mr. Crosbie where to get off.

Patricia invited me over to a dinner party at the Farmhouse. I couldn't think why at first but it soon became clear. Patricia was doing some matchmaking. Margaret had no idea I'd been invited. Margaret still hadn't forgiven me for Valentine's Day. I'd tried to make things OK, but she wouldn't believe I wasn't out with Chris that night.

Trouble is, I can't tell her the truth and it looks as if she might have a reason to be jealous. I'm not going to be unfaithful, but I *am* tempted. Mick Johnson from the pizza parlour and his girlfriend were there too. A really odd mix. Even Mum noticed I hadn't seen that much of Margaret.

It was a peculiar evening. We small talked the night away, except when Max got on to his soap box about the National Health. As if I'd work for the private sector. I'll leave that to the public school lot in my year. Everything we said seemed to be Significant. Patricia and Max exchanged glances whenever Margaret and I spoke to each other. Max was obviously in on the secret, especially when he put his foot in it about "trendy lefties and the gay rights crowd". He didn't know what to do with himself.

I found out what was going on afterwards.

Margaret had admitted to Patricia she and I are having an affair.

What really made me mad was Margaret telling anyone. I suddenly had this vision of Patricia casually dropping it into the conversation with Mum. Margaret turned on me and I can hardly blame her. But if anyone's going to tell Mum, I want it to be me. She'd get the wrong idea from someone else. I hate the thought of some neighbour knowing before she does. The way things are going though, it'll probably be in the papers soon.

There's nothing like a good row for getting things out into the open. We made it up, friends again.

2nd March 1994

Last night, I slept with Chris.

Chris invited me to a uni debate. I was supposed to be going for a drink with Margaret. I should have invited her too, but I didn't want to.

The debate was brilliant and Chris was the star. There was this arrogant MP pontificating about how government policy was the best thing that could have happened to the NHS. Chris tore him to shreds. She had all the facts and figures at her fingertips. He was left opening and closing his mouth like a goldfish. I wish it had been question time or something like that. She made him look a complete idiot.

It's not only that she knows her stuff. She listens to what people say and answers them. This stupid MP didn't. All he could do was to spout the official line. Then, when Chris pointed out some obvious discrepancy, he spouted it again. She ought to go into parliament herself. With her as Minister of Health, we'd have hospitals to be proud of.

Chris invited me back to her place with a load of her other friends. That's another thing about her. She's incredibly popular. Not just with the students, the staff get on with her as well – even some of the reactionary ones. I think she draws the line at Tory MPs, though!

I love being around her. She makes me feel so alive. And intelligent. I was the only first year there, but Chris always acts as if my opinions are just as important and valid as anyone else's. She can be quite cutting if someone's patronising.

We all talked for hours. Somehow, I ended up outstaying everyone else. Chris wanted me to. I helped wash up. When we were alone, I told her about Margaret letting the cat out of the bag to Patricia. We talked about being gay and what it means. The trouble with Margaret is she doesn't take our relationship seriously. Even when she gets jealous. I suppose she must be bisexual. She enjoys being with me and sleeping with me, as far as we go, but as far as she's concerned, we're not a couple. I want a girlfriend I can show off, go out with, be seen with. Perhaps not everywhere, though – Brookside Close couldn't take it.

It's all a game, a pretence, to Margaret. Sooner or later, she'll grow out of it, get married and settle down. I don't want that. Over the past few weeks, I've come to realise I'll never be happy that way. Chris said maybe I *will* grow out of it. When she said that, I knew for certain I won't.

Chris invited me to stay.

There was the sofa.

Or there was her bed.

I chose her bed.

It was a revelation! I enjoyed making love with Peter, but with Chris it felt right, natural. Perhaps it's because she's a woman. Whatever turns me on is likely to do the same for her.

Chris made me laugh – right in the middle of all this passion! In the morning, Chris was like she always is, casual, bright and cheerful.

Mum was worried when I didn't come back. She assumed I was round at Margaret's, where I usually am. Only Margaret came looking for me. I'm getting myself tied up in knots. I told them I'd stayed with a girl from my course called Jocelyn. It was the first name I could think of. Margaret looked as if she didn't believe me. I could hardly blame her – I sounded shifty even to myself.

Margaret went off in a huff. I told Mum we'd quarrelled because I forgot I was supposed to be going for a drink with her. Mum said what a pity and that was that. What should I do about Margaret, though? I'm not sure if I really want to go out with her any longer. It's not that I don't love her. I do. But being with her is so frustrating. It's like being in a cage, where you can't move because of the bars and because somebody's always watching.

4th March 1994

I couldn't just leave it with Chris. I waited for her and she asked me back to her flat. The first thing she said was that she doesn't normally sleep with her students. I was floored by that. It had completely slipped my mind that she was a lecturer. If she'd been a man, I would have been really on my guard. I'd have probably been screaming exploitation, but with Chris, it's not a power thing. She could still get into trouble if it came out, of course.

Was it a one night stand? Chris said it wasn't, but that doesn't necessarily mean we're an item. We could become one. I found myself really hoping that we would. I was dying to go back to bed with her. I'd be so proud to have her as a partner. I can just imagine myself living here.

Take it slow. That was Chris' message. It's sensible, but I want to fling myself into it all. She does want to start a relationship, though.

What should I do about Margaret?

We were talking about it when the bell rang. Talk about bad timing – it was her. She'd actually come to see Chris to ask if there was something going on between us! Chris was dead embarrassed. She tried to stop her finding out I was there, but I couldn't go on lying. It wasn't fair on Margaret. She deserves much better than that. I told her that I had been seeing Chris and that I had spent the night at her flat.

Margaret went mad. There was nothing I could say to defend myself. She said I'd used her. I didn't mean to. When I opened my mouth, nothing came out. What could I say?

It's as if my affair with Margaret was like a rehearsal. Not real. I thought it was just her, but now I wonder if I was doing it too. Maybe I *was* using her. I've never felt so bad about myself in my entire life. Margaret said our relationship was the worst mistake she'd ever made. Her parting shot was that she hoped one day she'd meet somebody normal. She knows just how to hurt me.

This *is* normal for me. It feels right. It feels genuine. I didn't mean to use Margaret. None of it was conscious. The thing I feared most right from the beginning has happened. I've lost my best friend.

9th March 1994

I met Margaret in the Parade today. We've been avoiding each other. I really wanted to talk to her. Even though I've got Chris, I miss Margaret.

But the more I get to know Chris, the better I like her. If this carries on, I'll want to use the word love. But she isn't Margaret. We're not so evenly matched. Chris is all for equality in a relationship, but there's nothing either of us can do about the fact she's older and more experienced than me. Maybe when I've done a lot more thinking and studying, I'll be on her level.

How can Margaret simply ignore me? As if I don't exist. She just said that's how she wants it. Fine! I tried to meet her half way, but there's a limit.

The Keith episode is repeating itself. She's found herself a fella. A real macho man. A soldier, of all people. His name's Carl – his Mum and Dad are moving in next door. What's she trying to prove? As if I didn't know.

I sat in my room and fumed about her. I couldn't just leave

it, so I went round to have it out. We rowed. What else could I expect? She said she'd have come to her senses soon enough, even if Chris hadn't come along. Who's to say she's being sensible now? But she can't bear the thought of being gay. The only people she's interested in sexually – so she says – are men. That wasn't true a few weeks ago. She can deny it as much as she likes. Her fear is blotting out her feelings.

Chris didn't agree. Which annoyed me a bit. She said if you draw a line between gay and straight, most people are nearer to the middle than they find comfortable. That's true enough. I'm still confused as to why I found Peter attractive. I can't deny that I did. Also, Margaret and I are both young. I hate it when she says that, but I suppose she might be right in this case. We were experimenting together. For me, it was a way of putting a toe out of the closet. Even now, I don't know if I should risk a whole foot.

16th March 1994

I saw Margaret sneak away from Carl's tonight. It was pretty obvious what she'd been doing. I thought I'd got her out of my system. The other night, I caught them kissing on the Close. Margaret made sure I saw them. She was really putting on an act. I wonder if she's told him about us. Probably not. Soldier boy wouldn't be able to handle it.

They don't go round together in the day time. There's definitely something funny going on. Margaret's too busy trying to prove how normal she is to notice. I asked her what she was up to. I couldn't believe her reaction. Told me to stop being so high and mighty. At least, her relationship's with a fella.

She told me to mind my own business. What could I say? What she does now is up to her.

26th March 1994

Term's over and I'm stuck at home – when I'm not staying with Chris. Mum thought she'd see a bit more of me in the holidays. Especially since Margaret and I don't go around together any more. I felt really guilty. I want to tell her about me and Chris, but I'm just not ready to yet. Chris has a great relationship with her parents, and it still took a lot for her to come out to them.

The big hurdle is Chris' job. Even if Mum *could* handle me possibly being gay, she'd go berserk if she thought I was sleeping with one of the lecturers. The trouble is, once you start lying, it's impossible to stop. I covered up by going on about how much work I've got to do. Which is true.

Mum suggested I invite Chris round for tea. Part of me wanted to do it. Maybe if they met and liked each other, it wouldn't be so bad. Maybe I'm dreaming. I'd be tempted if Chris came around.

31st March 1994

Rachel was fifteen yesterday. Mum and I tried to make her birthday as special as possible. I couldn't help thinking how disastrous her last one was. Mum was determined that everything be back to normal. As if anything in this house could be normal. She made some very pointed comments about my staying away all the time. She'd forgotten I live here.

Maybe I should move out. Not in with Chris, of course. That would be wonderful, but asking for trouble. I could share a place nearer uni perhaps. I don't know where I'd find the money for the rent, though. My grant won't cover it because we live so close. But I can dream.

Sinbad came with a present for Rachel. I haven't seen him for ages. He asked me if it was all over between me and Margaret. As if he didn't know. I should think he could give me chapter and verse on Margaret's latest affair if I asked him. Which I didn't. I told him there was someone else. I didn't say who. He'd only get worried if he knew Chris was a lecturer. I just said it was a friend from university.

I feel so far away from my family. I was standing in the corner of the kitchen watching Rachel blowing out her candles. It was like they were part of another world. My real life is the one I live at uni and with Chris. Is this being gay? Or is it growing up?

6th April 1994

I had a surprise visitor today. Margaret. She hasn't spoken to me for weeks. I was really pleased to see her, which proves I must have got over our break up.

But when she told me her news, I was – well, gob-smacked. She's only got back together with Derek. They're going to ride off into the Bosnian sunset. Of course, I had a million questions to ask her. Like why Derek? What happened to Carl? Is she on the rebound? From Carl, if not from me.

She's decided Derek is the one for her. Always has been. For life. It's fate. I wasn't wild about being described as a mistake. What about our relationship? That must have meant something to her. She couldn't just ignore it. Pretend it never happened.

That's precisely what she wants to do. Her exact words were "I'm going to put it behind me". I hurt her very badly when I went off with Chris. I wish I hadn't done it. She was supposed to be my best friend. I always promised myself I'd be absolutely straight in relationships. Finish one before starting another.

On the other hand, Chris always said Margaret would survive and she has. How could I be sad for her when she was so happy and excited? Margaret's view was that I've got Chris and she's got Derek. Why can't we be glad for each other? I couldn't let Margaret go off with all this hurt and bitterness between us – for a while we really meant something to each other. I went over to the Farnham's, she was just packing, ready to go.

We hugged and I wished her the best of luck. Then the tears started, both of us! Streaming down our faces. And then she was gone, just like that. Like it never happened – but it did. At least we parted friends.

When she'd left, I found the scarf she gave me for Christmas and put it on. It still smells of her perfume. I never gave her anything she could keep. She probably wouldn't want it in any case. She may try to forget, but I'm going to remember. Margaret was my first love and my first best friend. There'll never be anyone else like her.

THE END